"Silver Sands, Just Like I Said."

He gestured around them. "The moon and stars are transforming the beach into silver sands. That is one beautiful sight. I can picture a ship out there with tall masts and a crow's nest. And here comes the pirate to claim his maiden. He's wearing his bed-sheet shirt, of course."

"Of course," Lisa said, smiling in spite of herself.

Cam shifted to face her, and she stared at him with wide eyes, her heart racing. The almost eerie luminescence from the heavenly spectacle cast flickering shadows and silvery hues over Cam, making him appear even bigger, darker, more powerful.

"Lisa."

"Oh, dear heaven," she whispered, then lifted her arms to encircle his neck.

Cam moved one hand to the nape of her neck, the other to the small of her back, then pulled her up against him, his mouth sweeping down on hers.

Dear Reader,

Welcome to Silhouette! Our goal is to give you hours of unbeatable reading pleasure, and we hope you'll enjoy each month's six new Silhouette Desires. These sensual, provocative love stories are both believable and compelling—sometimes they're poignant, sometimes humorous, but always enjoyable.

Indulge yourself. Experience all the passion and excitement of falling in love along with our heroine as she meets the irresistible man of her dreams and together they overcome all obstacles in the path to a happy ending.

If this is your first Desire, I hope it'll be the first of many. If you're already a Silhouette Desire reader, thanks for your support! Look for some of your favorite authors in the coming months: Stephanie James, Diana Palmer, Dixie Browning, Ann Major and Doreen Owens Malek, to name just a few.

Happy reading!

Isabel Swift
Senior Editor

SDRL-7/85

ROBIN ELLIOTT
Silver Sands

Silhouette Desire

Published by Silhouette Books New York

America's Publisher of Contemporary Romance

SILHOUETTE BOOKS
300 East 42nd St., New York, N.Y. 10017

Copyright © 1987 by Joan Elliott Pickart

ISBN: 0-373-05362-2

First Silhouette Books printing July 1987

America's Publisher of Contemporary Romance

Printed in the U.S.A.

ROBIN ELLIOTT

lives in Arizona with her husband and three daughters. Formerly employed in a high school library, she is now devoting her time to writing romance novels. She also writes under her own name, Joan Elliott Pickart.

For my Aunt Elsie,
and the fond memories of Mark Twain

One

Lisa Peterson scowled at the neat row of words before her, then made a face at the white letters on the green computer screen. She got up out of the soft leather chair and began to pace, her bare feet sinking into the chocolate-colored carpeting. Her full lips were pursed in concentration and her green eyes were slightly cloudy, an indication that she was troubled.

She flopped onto the yellow flowered sofa, stretched her tanned legs out in front of her, and in the next instant was up and moving again. In white shorts and a blue T-shirt with an enormous question mark stenciled on the front, she appeared younger than her twenty-six years.

With thudding steps Lisa left the room and went down the hall and across the living room, which was decorated in earth tones. Her destination was the yellow-and-white kitchen, where she poured herself a glass of iced tea, then marched back to stand once more in front of the computer. She sighed, pushed several buttons, and the machine hummed, signaling that the words on the screen would be saved on a disk.

"Big deal," she muttered.

The transfer completed, Lisa removed the disk from the disk drive and slipped it into its protective cardboard envelope. She lifted the telephone receiver, fitted it into a special device, then sat down again in her chair.

Lisa decided she'd pour out her woes to Bret. He always left his computer on, so even if he wasn't home, she could communicate through their modem hookup. If he was out, she'd instruct the computer to print the message so he'd see it when he came back. Maybe it would help her get past this stubborn part of her book if she talked to someone, even if that someone was a computer. Her characters simply weren't cooperating, and for two cents she'd toss the lusty, handsome pirate and his swooning maiden into the ocean.

With a decisive nod, Lisa typed the code that would activate Bret's computer and prepare it to receive her dispatch. A small green square blinked at her from the corner of the screen, indicating that she could proceed.

ARE YOU THERE, MY SWEET? she typed.

Lisa plunked her elbow on the desk top, cupped her chin in her hand, frowned at the screen, and waited.

Cam Porter jerked in surprise when the computer he'd been bending over and peering at suddenly beeped three times, then produced a line of white letters. His gaze swept over the expensive equipment and he nodded in comprehension.

"Modem hookup," he said under his breath. "Classy." He sank into the chair in front of the computer. "Why not?" He smiled, crinkling the corners of his dark eyes and flashing his white teeth, which contrasted with his deeply tanned skin. He lifted his large hands to the keyboard.

YES, he typed with long fingers, I'M HERE.

THANK GOODNESS, came the reply moments later. I'M A DAMSEL IN DISTRESS.

Ho-ho, Cam thought. Bret had a modem hookup going with a woman. Maybe he should tell her Bret wasn't home. On the other hand, he really should see if he could help her. Let it not be said that Cameron Porter didn't assist damsels in distress.

WHAT'S WRONG? he typed, then slouched back in the chair to await the reply. He laced his hands behind his head, thick, black hair as dark as his eyes falling over his fingers. The casual motion caused the muscles in his arms and his wide shoulders to bunch beneath his open-necked blue shirt. Faded jeans pulled tightly over corded thighs as he stretched his long legs out in front of him. "Well, honey," he said aloud, "are you going to tell me or not?"

As if it had heard him, the computer hummed again, white letters dancing across the screen in rapid succession.

I FIZZLED OUT IN THE MIDDLE OF A KISS. FROZE UP, the dispatch read. THIS ONE WAS TO LEAD TO SEX. IT'S TIME TO GO TO BED WITH HIM AND POOF! NOTHING. ANY SUGGESTIONS?

Cam dropped his hands to the arms of the chair and sat straight up, ramrod stiff, eyes widening as he stared at the screen.

"What in the hell?" he said. What was Bret doing, playing amateur shrink in his spare time?

WELL? the computer demanded.

I'M THINKING, Cam typed.

TAKE ALL THE TIME YOU NEED. I'LL JUST SIT HERE AND HAVE A NERVOUS BREAK-DOWN.

"Oh, Lord," Cam said, running his hand down his face. The woman sounded desperate. He'd better tell her he wasn't Bret. No, she might be pushed over the edge if she thought there was no one to help her in her moment of need. But what was he going to say to her? Think, Porter!

Lisa sipped her iced tea and nodded approvingly. She felt better already. Just telling Bret that she'd hit a block in her writing had helped immensely. The crummy kiss was the pirate's fault. There was nothing romantic about kissing the living daylights out of a woman on the deck of a ship while being soaked to the skin by cold, smelly sea water. He should take her to his cabin first and . . .

The computer beeped for her attention.

MAYBE YOU'RE BEING TOO HARD ON YOURSELF, the message read. COULD BE THAT THE GUY WAS A LOUSY KISSER. IT CALLS FOR A CERTAIN EXPERTISE ON HIS PART, YOU KNOW.

THAT'S THE CONCLUSION I JUST CAME TO, Lisa typed, her fingers flying over the keyboard. THE SETTING WAS WRONG. I'LL MOVE RIGHT

INTO THE BEDROOM, THEN DO LIPS ON LIPS, LEADING TO BODY ON BODY. THANKS FOR YOUR HELP.

WAIT! came the almost instantaneous reply.

WAIT FOR WHAT? Lisa answered, frowning slightly.

ARE YOU SURE YOU WANT TO TAKE THIS STEP? HAVE YOU THOUGHT IT THROUGH?

YOU'RE SO CUTE, Lisa typed, laughing softly. THE HECK WITH VIRTUE. GO FOR THE GUSTO. I'M SIGNING OFF NOW. I WANT TO GET BACK TO IT WHILE I'M HOT TO TROT. SEE YOU SOON.

Cameron frantically pushed the keys on the computer before the connection was severed, then sighed with relief when the printer was activated. He was so shook up, he'd never remember everything he'd said to that woman. This way, he decided, he'd have both sides of the conversation in printed form when he confessed to Bret. Hot to trot? What had he done? The heck with virtue? He'd sent a virgin scrambling into some joker's bed? The guy was even a lousy kisser, which meant he was probably a real zero as a lover. That woman's psyche could be warped for life.

"Damn it," Cam said, raking his hand through his hair as he got to his feet. The printer stopped, and he tore off the perforated paper, scanning the words. "Oh, brother," he moaned, shaking his head. "She's going to do it. Maybe she's doing it right now."

The sound of the front door opening brought Cam striding from the room that housed the computer, the printout clutched tightly in his hand.

"Cam," a man said. "It's great to see you. Five years is a helluva long time."

"It sure is," Cam said, shaking hands vigorously with the other man. "Too long. Bret, I've got to talk to you."

"You bet," Bret said, whomping him on the shoulder. "We've got a lot of catching up to do. I see you found the key to the house all right. Had a beer?" he said, starting toward the kitchen.

"No," Cam said, following close behind. "Bret, listen, I was looking at your computer setup and—"

"Top-notch equipment," Bret said, opening the refrigerator and taking out two cans of beer.

"Yeah," Cam said, accepting one of the drinks. "Thing is, a message came in over the modem, and I answered it."

"Oh?" Bret said, going back into the living room. He sank onto the sofa and looked at Cam. "And?"

"I blew it," Cam said. "Whoever your weird friend is, I sent her straight into some guy's bed. Here," he said, shoving the printout at Bret. "Read this."

Bret's eyes flickered over the paper, then he took a deep swallow of beer to hide his smile. He coughed roughly to disguise his laughter, then plastered a serious expression on his face.

"My, my," he said, "I do believe she's gone and done it."

"How old is she?" Cam said, settling into a chair.

"Oh, eighteen or nineteen, I imagine."

"Sweet heaven," Cam said, rolling his eyes in the direction of the designated place. "She's just a kid. She sounded so bummed out, I told her it was probably his fault and... Who is this girl?"

"She lives down the coast a few miles, has a nice place, beachfront property in Malibu."

"Bret, your friend, your virginal friend, is in bed with a man at this very moment."

"Yeah, and he's the swashbuckler type—a pirate. I'd bet money on it. A rogue, as they say."

"We've got to get down there," Cam said.

"It's a little late to go charging to the rescue, don't you think?"

"We can't just sit here, Bret," Cam said, getting to his feet. "What if the guy is a sicko or—Don't you care about this girl?"

Bret placed his hand over his heart. "I love her like a sister," he said dramatically. "Okay," he added, "we'll drive down there. Maybe she'll go out with us for some dinner. It's that time of day. Let's go."

He coughed again to camouflage his laughter as the two men left the house and got into Bret's sleek sports car.

"It really is great to see you, Cam," Bret said as he whipped through the traffic. "I hope you know that while you're here I'm going to do a number on you and convince you to work with me. Aren't you tired of playing *I Spy* all over the world for the government?"

"I don't know," Cam said, shrugging. "I need a vacation, that's for sure. This last assignment was rough. There's nothing in my job description as a computer expert for the Feds that says I have to dodge bullets. I nearly got my head blown off over there."

"Where were you?"

"That's classified info, but it wasn't a tourist attraction, I'll tell you that. I was mad as hell about the danger they put me and my crew in. They're walking on eggshells around me right now. Month off with pay, car at my disposal—the works. Can't you drive any faster?''

"I'm above the speed limit now," Bret said. "So, you're thinking things over about your job."

"Yeah, I need to cool off, view it objectively."

"You do that," Bret said, nodding. "Then tell them to take a flying leap, and come work for me. No, not *for* me. With me. I'm offering you a full partnership in Peterson Computer Corporation."

"You have a partner," Cam said. "Peterson Computer Corporation. Bret and Lisa Peterson. You told me your sister was coming into the company as soon as she graduated from college."

"She did. Lisa is one of the best program writers in the business. She helped put us on the map. She left Peterson Computer two years ago, though."

"Why? She get married or something?"

"No, she needed a change, that's all. I've hired good people, Cam, but I've got more work than I can handle. The partnership is yours if you want it."

"Well, I . . ."

"No, don't say anything now. Just think about it. You and I go back a long way, Cam. How the army survived us during our stint, I'll never know. The fact that we haven't seen each other in five years doesn't change our friendship one iota. I feel as though I saw you yesterday. You look like hell, I might add."

"Oh, thanks," Cam said, chuckling. "You're good for my ego."

"You're tired. Not just physically, either."

"Yeah," Cam said quietly, "I'm tired. I feel more like eighty-four than thirty-four."

"Are we thirty-four already? Damn, we are. I must be having fun, 'cause time sure is flying."

"Knowing you, you're bed-hopping up and down the coast of California."

"You're no slouch in that department, Porter," Bret said, smiling. "You've had your share of women."

"Well, I've never touched an eighteen-year-old virgin. Are we nearly at that girl's house?"

"Yep, it's just up ahead."

"Malibu Beach. She's got bucks, huh?"

"She does all right."

"So do you, apparently," Cam said. "Your house isn't exactly shabby, and this car is something."

"Compliments of Peterson Computer Corporation, buddy—half of which can be yours."

"We'll see, Bret. I need to get my head on straight before I make any decisions about my future. I'll rest, relax, then decide what I want to do."

"Fair enough. Well," Bret said, pulling up next to a brightly lit house, "we're here. This ought to be very interesting."

"I feel like an idiot," Cam said, getting out of the car and walking around to join Bret. "I don't even know this girl. We're not going to be too popular if she's decided she doesn't need rescuing from the lousy kisser. Is that her car?"

"Yep."

"Maybe lover boy split already. Bret, you go talk to her. She doesn't need a stranger on her doorstep if she's upset."

"No way," Bret said, shaking his head. "It was your conversation with her over the modem that got her hot to trot, remember?"

"Hell," Cam said, striding toward the house. Bret coughed again. "You ought to do something about that cough," Cam said over his shoulder.

"It'll be fine in a few minutes," Bret said, grinning at Cam's broad back.

Lisa had just sliced a banana onto the thick layer of peanut butter on the bread when the knock sounded at the door. She popped a piece of banana into her mouth and padded out of the kitchen. She straightened her T-shirt over the waistband of her shorts, and went to answer the summons.

A smile lit up her face when she opened the door. "Bret," she said, "what a nice sur—"

In the next instant, Bret had grabbed her around the waist and pressed her head to his chest, cutting off her welcoming speech.

"Oh, my poor little tulip," he said. "My innocent blossom. Are you all right? No, of course you're not. Where is that cad? Cam and I are going to tear him limb from limb."

"Cam? Cam who? What are you talking about?" Lisa mumbled into his shirt. "Let me go!"

"Feel free to cry, my rosebud," Bret rambled on. "Pour out your misery. I told you about Cam Porter, remember? Army buddy? You just never had a chance to meet him. Actually, my petunia, it was Cam who answered your message when it came over the modem. He feels very responsible for the present state of your virtue and insisted we come right over and check on you. Wasn't that thoughtful of him? It certainly was."

Bret slowly released his hold on Lisa, and she looked up at him. When he winked at her, she nearly burst out laughing, but managed to keep a straight face. She quickly replayed in her mind the messages relayed back and forth on the computer, and her green eyes danced with merriment.

Cam, whoever he was, thought the whole thing was on the level, she realized. Cam Porter. Yes, she remembered Bret talking about him. He must be standing in the doorway, but since Bret was six feet tall to her five foot five, she couldn't see the mysterious Cam. This was hysterical! The man actually believed she'd called for help on the computer, then hopped into bed with her crummy kisser. Oh, what a funny bit. It wasn't going to last long, though. Once this Cam got a good look at her, he'd see she was Bret's sister. But in the meantime...

"Oh-h-h," Lisa wailed, covering her face with her hands and moving out of Bret's arms. "I'm a fallen woman, a wanton hussy, a—a whole bunch of other stuff."

"What can I say," Bret said solemnly, throwing up his hands. "Play the game, earn the name."

"Oh-h-h!"

"Damn it, Bret," Cam said, slamming the door, "that was a rotten way to put it."

Lisa peered through her fingers at the tall figure who was scowling at her brother, and her breath caught in her throat. She'd heard about Cam Porter for years, but she'd had no idea he looked like *that*. He was the most blatantly masculine man she had ever seen. He had such rugged, tanned features, such wide shoulders, such... Oh, dear, she was forgetting her role.

"Oh-h-h!"

"Look, miss," Cam said, "take it easy, okay? Everything will be fine. Right, Bret?"

"Beats me," Bret said, shrugging. "Depends on whether or not the jerk writes her phone number on rest-room walls."

"For crying out loud, Peterson," Cam roared. "Don't you have a sympathetic bone in your body?"

"Nobody sympathized with me when I lost my virginity," Bret said, thumping himself on the chest. "And I was only—"

"Shame on you, Bret," Lisa said, still peering at Cam through her fingers. "If Mom knew, she'd—uh-oh."

Cam narrowed his eyes as he looked at a grinning Bret, then reached out and grasped Lisa's wrists, pulling her hands away from her face. He glanced at her sparkling green eyes, then Bret's, her strawberry-blond hair, then Bret's, and nodded slowly.

"Lisa Peterson, I presume?" Cam said, a smile tugging at his lips.

"Hi," she said, laughing out loud. "How's life?"

Bret fell apart. He laughed until he couldn't breathe, then collapsed on the sofa. Cam grinned and shook his head.

What a smile, Lisa thought, gazing up at Cam as he watched Bret. It softened his features and... He was the same age as Bret, but he looked harder, more worldly, as though he'd fought many a battle in his life. Oh, why hadn't she paid more attention when Bret had blithered on about Cameron Porter? Where had he been? What was he doing there now?

"Can you put a cork in him?" Cam said, shifting his gaze to Lisa. "Your eyes are beautiful."

"They're the same color as Bret's," she said, hoping her voice was steadier than it sounded to her own ears.

"He just looks like a green-eyed cat on the prowl. But you? Must be the face surrounding the eyes that makes the difference. It's a pleasure to meet you, Lisa," Cam said, extending his hand, "even if you do have a nutty brother."

"Well, I did go along with the joke," she said, placing her hand in his. "You're a good sport, Cam." His hand was strong. And warm. Callused, too, but gentle. *Very* warm, and the heat was traveling up her arm, across her breasts, and— Enough. "Bret," she said, pulling her hand free and walking to the sofa, "zip it, for heaven's sake."

"I love it, I love it," Bret said, clutching his stomach. "I couldn't believe it when Cam told me about— oh, man!"

"Just what was your computer message all about, Lisa?" Cam said.

"My book," she said, smiling at him. "I write historical romance novels, and I was stuck on a scene. Sometimes it helps to talk it over a bit with someone. Bret and I chat all the time with the modem, so I took a chance that he might be home and called for help. Please, sit down, Cam," she said, sinking onto the sofa next to Bret.

Cam sat opposite them in a soft leather chair, and frowned.

"You left Peterson Computer to write romance novels?" he said, his frown deepening.

"Yes," she said, looking at him steadily, "I did."

"But didn't you graduate from MIT with a degree in engineering and computer science?"

"Yes," she said, lifting her chin a little higher.

"I see," Cam said. But he really didn't. What was a brilliant woman like Lisa Peterson doing writing romantic fluff? She'd walked away from a partnership with Bret at Peterson Computer to live in a fantasy world of pirates and ravished maidens?

"I was going to suggest we all go out to dinner," Bret said, "but if Cam sinks any lower in that chair, he's going to fall asleep."

Cam chuckled. "You're right," he said. "I've crossed so many time zones in the past twenty-four hours I don't know if it's yesterday, today or tomorrow. I'm afraid I wouldn't be very good company."

"Well, we'll catch up on all the news after you've had some sleep," Bret said, getting to his feet. "We'll go home, grab a sandwich, and you can hit the sack."

"Sounds great," Cam said, pushing himself up. "Another five minutes in that chair and you would have had me for the night, Lisa."

Interesting thought, she mused. "You're staying with Bret?" she said, rising to join them.

"He sure is," Bret said.

"For now," Cam said. "I sent Bret a telegram and said I was on my way. I'm what is known as an uninvited guest."

"And a welcome one," Bret said. "Come on, buddy, let's pour your decrepit body into bed."

Decrepit body? Lisa thought, suppressing a smile. If that was decrepit, her nervous system would never stand the shock when he was rested up and raring to go. How could a tired man exude such raw virility, such an aura of authority? And those eyes. Deep ebony pools of... Heavens, she was getting fanciful.

"Let's plan on dinner tomorrow night," Bret said. "All right with you, Lisa?"

"Yes, fine. Sounds like fun."

"Well, Lisa Peterson," Cam said, extending his hand, "it certainly was interesting meeting you."

"I hope you're not angry about our little joke," she said, smiling as she placed her hand in his.

"Not at all," he said, returning the smile. "I trust the kiss and subsequent events went well?"

"Oh, yes, no problem," she said. There was that heat from his hand again, and it was zinging right through her. Was he stroking her wrist with his thumb? He was, and he knew it, the rat. He wasn't so tired he didn't know what he was doing. "Sleep well, Mr. Porter," she said, slipping her hand free.

"See ya, kid," Bret said, giving her a peck on the cheek.

"Yeah," Cam said, "see ya." And then he winked at her.

"Bye," Lisa said as Bret closed the door behind them. He'd winked at her! Did men actually still do that? How corny. Never mind that it was the sexiest wink she'd ever seen; even combined with that heart-stopping smile, it was still corny.

Cam Porter, Lisa mused, walking slowly back into the kitchen. Bret and Cam had been in the army together; that much she knew. When Bret had started Peterson Computer he'd spoken of Cam, said he was trying to get him to come into the new company. But Cam had been working for the government by then and had declined Bret's offer. Now here he was, out of the blue. Apparently, his decision to come had been very sudden. She assumed he was on vacation. For how long? Would he spend the time at Bret's?

"My goodness, you're nosy," Lisa said, slapping a slice of bread on top of her sandwich. She sounded like a teenager ogling her big brother's handsome friend, which she had done a time or two when she *was* a teenager.

Bret and Cam. What a pair, she thought, taking a bite of the sandwich. The women of Malibu were going to go nuts. Bret was too gorgeous for his own good, with his well-muscled physique, big green eyes, sun-bleached hair, and tan. And Cam? Cam, the pirate, with hair and eyes as black as the devil's, and a body that simply didn't quit. She might as well go out to dinner with them tomorrow night, before the hordes descended.

Lisa poured herself a glass of milk and carried her meager dinner into the living room, sinking onto the sofa with a sigh. Cam was going to push the issue of her leaving Peterson Computer, she could tell. The reference to her college degree, the edge to his voice when he spoke of her writing romance novels... She'd seen that reaction before; the disbelief, the disapproval. No one really understood except Bret. Their parents were still horrified at her career change, and were still waiting for her to come to her senses. Cam was probably quizzing Bret about it right now. Well, it was none of his business. And Bret would tell him that.

"So there, Cameron Porter," she said, with a decisive nod. "Go take a nap. And whether he's your friend or not, you keep your mouth shut, Bret."

As Bret maneuvered the sports car through the heavy traffic, he wasn't saying a word, due to the fact that Cam was sound asleep. Bret pulled into the driveway of his house, shut off the ignition, then got out of the car and walked around to the passenger side. He opened the door, poked Cam in the arm with his finger, then stepped quickly back.

"Cam," he said, "wake up."

"Mmm?"

"Come on, buddy. We're home."

"Mmm?"

"I'm going to get myself killed," Bret muttered. He reached into the car and placed his hand on Cam's shoulder. "Cam, we're ... aaagh!" he yelled as vise-like fingers closed over his wrist. "It's me, Bret. You're breaking my arm!"

"Oh, sorry," Cam said, jerking his hand away and blinking several times.

"I should have left you out here," Bret said, grinning and rubbing his wrist. "Waking a sleeping Cam Porter can be hazardous to one's health. I'll never forget the time you had that general slammed against the wall with your arm crushing his Adam's apple because he woke you. Poor guy. All he wanted was for you to drive him to the golf course."

Cam chuckled and unfolded himself from the car. "Reflexes, my boy," he said. "Sharp reflexes."

"Dangerous reflexes."

"They've kept me alive a time or two, before the army and since," he said, walking beside Bret to the house.

"You've told me about the befores," Bret said, unlocking the door. "What's happened since?"

"This and that," Cam said as they entered the living room. "I think I'll pass on the food, Bret. I'm too tired to chew."

"All right, get some sleep, lie around tomorrow, then the next day I'll show you Peterson Computer.

Oh, and don't forget we're having dinner with Lisa tomorrow night."

"She's a beautiful woman, Bret."

"Yep, she is."

"I can't understand why she'd... Never mind. My brain is mush. Nothing would make sense to me tonight. Listen, thanks for everything."

"What are friends for? Good night."

"Yeah. Good night."

A short time later Cam lay in his comfortable bed, staring up into the darkness. He'd taken a quick shower, then crawled naked between the cool sheets, hours of sleep his fervent wish.

Man, he was tired, wiped out, he thought, running his hand over his face. And not just physically. Bret had seen further than that, too, so apparently it showed. Friends like Bret were rare, he thought. Cam pops up after five years, and Bret welcomes him into his home as though he's only been gone a week. And what a swanky home. Peterson Computer was going places. Peterson Computer Corporation. Bret and Lisa. Lisa Peterson. That was one beautiful woman. She wasn't very big, sort of reminded him of a china doll with her big green eyes and feathery curls. But she was feisty, had that stubborn set to her chin like Bret, and obviously had a sense of humor. Lord, her eyes sparkled like emeralds when she was laughing that wind-chime laugh of hers.

The big question mark on her T-shirt, Cam mused. That fit her... a question mark. Why had she left Peterson Computer to write that junk? It apparently wasn't a passing fancy if she'd been at it for two years. Had she gotten her crazy pirates published, or was she just messing around? A degree from MIT, and she was spending her time writing sex scenes and sword fights, or whatever pirates did. Weird. Yeah, the T-shirt fit. Literally, too, right over full breasts he had definitely noticed, along with shapely legs and a cute little—

"Lord," Cam muttered with a snort of disgust. Lisa was his best friend's sister, for crying out loud. There was an unspoken code regarding these types of situations. A man didn't hit on his best friend's sister. He was going to be the perfect gentleman around Miss Peterson. But she sure was beautiful.

"Go to sleep, Porter," he said to the night.

With a weary sigh, Cam closed his eyes, and in the next moment was dead to the world, deep in a dreamless sleep.

At one o'clock the next afternoon Lisa wandered out onto her redwood deck and sank onto a padded chaise lounge. She'd worked steadily since dawn, and she needed a break. She'd eaten an unimaginative lunch and planned to enjoy her picture-perfect view of the ocean before going back to the computer. The book was ahead of schedule, and if she didn't hit any more glitches, it would be winging its way to her New York agent within the next week or so. Her agent, her editor, everyone would be pleased. Jasmine Peters would have done it again.

"What a name," Lisa said, laughing softly. "Jasmine." The pseudonym had kept her parents from going into total cardiac arrest over her novels. It had been a compromise on her part when she'd sold the first book. The one she was finishing was her fifth, and she was contracted for three more. Jasmine Peters had arrived.

And Lisa Peterson? she mused, suddenly frowning. How was *she* doing? She had everything she could possibly want or need. She could check things off on her fingers and find nothing lacking in her life. Then why that niggling little feeling of late that something was missing, that there was a hollow space, a void, in her existence? That was ridiculous. As it was, there weren't enough hours in the day to keep up with her writing, friends, her busy social life. There was neither room nor desire to add anything.

Lisa sat up straighter in the lounge and gave herself a firm mental directive to knock off her silly, rambling thoughts. A blur in the distance on the beach caught her attention, and she shielded her eyes against the sun with her hand. It was a jogger thudding steadily in her direction.

"That's cute," Lisa mumbled. "This entire stretch is private beach."

The jogger continued to advance, and Lisa's heart suddenly did a strange flip-flop. Cam, her mind whispered. It was Cam. So? Why the skittering pulse? Why the flush she could definitely feel on her cheeks? A man was a man, for Pete's sake. Well, on a scale of ten, Cam was a twenty, but big deal. He must have run all the way from Bret's, which meant he was in good shape. Was he *ever* in good shape. *Oh, stop!*

Lisa pushed herself to her feet and walked to the railing of the deck as Cam closed the distance between them. She watched the fascinating play of his well-defined muscles as he ran in a smooth, steady motion. He was wearing cutoffs and a T-shirt, and the exposed parts of his tanned body glistened with perspiration.

An unwelcome surge of heat traveled through Lisa, and she tightened her hold on the railing as Cam stopped. He planted his hands on his hips, smiled up at her where she stood on the deck and looked at her for a moment, a very long moment, before he spoke.

"Hello, Lisa," he said finally, slightly out of breath from his run.

"Hello, Cam," she said, acutely aware that her heart was racing as though *she* had been jogging. And acutely aware of every rugged, masculine inch of the man standing below her.

"Can I talk you out of a glass of water before I head back?" Cam said.

"Sure. Come on up. Would you like iced tea, lemonade, a beer?"

"Just water, thanks," he said, heading for the stairs. "Here I am again, dropping in uninvited on a Peterson." He reached the deck and crossed to where Lisa stood. "Am I disturbing you?" he asked, his voice low, as he looked directly into her green eyes. "Am I, Lisa?"

Two

No. No, I was taking a break," Lisa said. She averted
her eyes from Cam's and plucked an imaginary thread
from the blue terry-cloth top she wore over pale blue
shorts.

How could a sweaty man smell so good? she wondered. It was the heady stuff of blatant "male." Cam
could bottle the stuff and make a fortune.

"I could get my own water," he said.

"What?" she said, looking up at him again. "Oh,
your water. I'll get it," she said, spinning around and
marching into the house. She gritted her teeth as the
sound of Cam's throaty chuckle floated in after her.
"Am I disturbing you?" she mimicked sarcastically in
the kitchen. Cute little innuendo there, Porter, she
fumed inwardly. The big lug knew he was good-
looking, knew he was dripping with sexuality. No
wonder Cam and Bret were best friends. They were

both lady-killers, bed-hoppers. A rotten thing to say about her own brother, but it was true.

Lisa thudded ice cubes into a glass with more force than necessary, filled the glass with water, then returned to the deck. At the doorway she stopped, stumbling slightly as she looked at Cam. He had turned to face the ocean, his arms spread wide along the railing, his large hands gripping the wood. One tennis shoe-clad foot was propped on the lowest rung. The April sun poured over him, causing his damp hair to glisten like polished ebony.

And Lisa saw it all. The wide set to his shoulders did not escape her, nor the corded muscles in his arms and legs. His stance shouted the virile, healthy masculinity of his massive body. Her gaze skimmed over him from head to toe, lingering on the faded material that hugged his buttocks.

Now she was getting hysterical, she thought. She didn't go around scrutinizing men's bottoms. Cameron Porter was going to drink his water, then get the heck off her deck so she could get back to work. This was ridiculous. She was gawking, for Pete's sake. What would she do next?

"Water," she said, crossing the deck.

"Oh, thanks," Cam said, taking the glass from her. He drained it in three swallows and handed it back.

"More?"

"No, that's plenty. Hit the spot," he said, turning to face the ocean again. "This is an incredible view. I can feel myself relaxing just standing here. It's peaceful, nearly hypnotizing."

Lisa set the glass on the table, then moved to the railing. "Yes, it's marvelous," she said. "Bret prefers to live a few blocks inland, as he likes to have a

lawn and trees, but I love this beach. I sit out here on
the deck whenever I have time. Did you recover from
your jet lag?''

"Yep, I'm as good as new."

"Where did you fly in from?"

"The other side of the world. Those sea gulls are
sassy, aren't they?" Cam said, smiling over at her.

"Yes," she said, matching his expression. "You
seem so impressed by all this, but I remember Bret
saying that the two of you spent time on the beach
during several of your leaves when you were in the
army."

"That seems like a million years ago," he said quietly, his gaze shifting to the waves lapping gently
against the sandy shore. "Bret and I were cocky young
soldiers then, ready to take on the world."

"And now?"

Cam turned, leaning back against the railing, his
arms crossed loosely over his broad chest. He frowned
for a long moment as he stared at the toe of his shoe,
then looked at Lisa with his dark eyes.

"The world has a way of taking a man on instead," he said. "I believe that's known as growing up
and facing reality. Things don't always go as we plan."

"No, they don't."

"Bret's dream has come true," Cam said, "but he's
worked hard for it."

"Yes, he has," Lisa said, nodding. "I'm happy for
him, and very proud. Peterson Computer has a fine
reputation, and Bret deserves the recognition he's
getting." Here it comes, she thought. Cam would start
quizzing her as to why she left the company to write
her novels. He'd edged into the subject very smoothly,
and now he was ready to pounce.

"Bret is showing me Peterson Computer Corporation tomorrow, and I'm looking forward to it. Oh, I have a message for you from Bret."

"I beg your pardon?" Lisa said, frowning slightly.

"He called just before I left the house for my run. He said to tell you, 'Seven, seafood, Suzanne.' I assume you understand that."

"Yes," she said. "Would you like to sit down?" He wasn't going to push her on why she'd left Peterson Computer? How strange. Well, he probably didn't care one way or the other, which was vaguely disappointing. "I have a few more minutes before I have to get back to work," she said, stretching out on the propped-up lounge chair.

Cam sat on a padded chair and placed one ankle over the other knee.

"Oh, Bret's message," Lisa said. "He didn't translate it for you?"

"No, he was rushing to a meeting. He said you'd explain. I mentioned I was going for a run, and he suggested I head this way and talk to you about the plans for tonight. So, here I am."

"Oh," she said. He'd been told to visit her, hadn't come on his own. There was that funny flutter of disappointment again. What was the matter with her? She didn't care a whit what Cameron Porter thought or did. "Bret said Suzanne?" she said, sitting up straighter.

"Seven, seafood, Suzanne," Cam said, checking the information off on his fingers.

Lisa frowned. "We're going at seven, having seafood at his favorite place on the wharf, so dress casually, and he's taking Suzanne as his date."

"It wasn't that tough a code to break," Cam said, smiling. "I had it pegged."

"Well, he could have gotten a date for you."

"I have one," he said, looking at her steadily. "Unless, of course, having me as your escort would create problems with a special man in your life."

"No, there's no one special, but, Cam, this is rather silly. There's no rule that says you have to drag along your best friend's little sister."

Cam laughed and shook his head. "Lisa, the problem will be trying to remember that you *are* my best friend's little sister. From where I'm sitting, you're a very beautiful woman, pure and simple."

The strange bubble of noise that erupted from her lips was definitely a giggle, and she felt the heat of a blush on her cheeks. Oh, no, she moaned silently, she couldn't believe this. It wasn't like her to behave like some childish dunderhead. What was this man doing to her?

"Time to get back to the green screen," she said, jumping to her feet.

"I'll get out of your way, then," Cam said, pushing himself up.

Lisa glanced at him and narrowed her eyes. He was laughing at her! He was grinning like the Cheshire cat, and those pirate eyes of his were dancing a merry jig. He'd flustered her, and he knew it. And he was enjoying every minute of it. What nerve.

"I'll see you at seven," he said, walking slowly toward her.

"Fine. Bye."

"Do I make you nervous for some reason?" he said, stopping directly in front of her.

"No, of course not," she said, tilting her head back to look at him. "Why would you make me nervous?"

"I thought maybe you'd picked up on the fact that I'd like to kiss you..." he said, his voice low. He trailed his thumb along the line of her jaw. Lisa shivered. "And it was making you nervous."

"No. I mean, no, I didn't realize that you wanted to...that is, I had no idea... Darn it, Cam, you've turned me into a blithering idiot. Go jog a few hundred miles or something."

Cam chuckled deep in his throat as he slid his hand to the nape of her neck. "I will," he said, lowering his head toward hers. "In a minute."

Move, Lisa's mind ordered her. Scream. Punch him in the nose. She had to do something, anything, because she couldn't let this man kiss her.

But he did.

Cam brushed his lips over Lisa's with such a fleeting motion that she registered what was now becoming the familiar emotion of disappointment. In the next instant he took full possession of her mouth, parting her lips and slipping his tongue into the dark sweetness to meet hers. His hand tightened slightly on her neck, and his arm slid around her waist, pulling her up against him. She inched her hands up his chest to circle his neck, and the kiss intensified.

Lisa seemed suspended in pleasure as she savored the taste, the feel, the aroma of Cameron Porter. A flash of desire swept through her unlike anything she had ever experienced before, and a soft moan escaped her throat. She leaned further into Cam's rugged contours.

This kiss, she mused dreamily, was sensational. It was also, she thought, her eyes popping open, not supposed to be happening.

"Cam," she said, pushing against his chest, "stop."

He lifted his head and gazed down at her, his dark eyes smoky with desire. "What?" he said, his voice raspy.

"Stop kissing me," she said, taking a steadying breath as she eased away from him.

"Why?"

Why? Lisa's mind echoed. She had no idea why. She could kiss Cam Porter for the next week straight and not bother to eat or sleep. She had never in her life registered such a startling reaction to a simple kiss. Simple? Ha! That was a kiss of practiced expertise, executed by a pro.

"I like kissing you," Cam said, smiling at her, "and you obviously like kissing me. Let's do it again," he said, reaching for her.

"No," she said, smacking his hand.

"Why?" he said, the smile broadening to a wide grin.

"Because . . . yes," she said, pointing a finger in the air, "because I'm Bret's little sister, remember?"

"Oh," he said, frowning. "Well, I did tell you I was going to have a problem with that. I have a tendency to see you as a beautiful, desirable, very kissable woman. You are, you know."

Oh, how sweet, Lisa thought. Now, wasn't that just the nicest thing to say? Oh, for Pete's sake, where was her common sense? Cam had his spiel down as smooth as glass. Did he think she was a nincompoop?

"Mr. Porter," she said, her hands on her hips, "I'm not some naive child. You and my brother are like peas in a pod, two of a kind."

"Am I being insulted?" he said, the smile back in place.

"I think so," she said, bursting into laughter. "I love Bret, but he is one fast hustler, let me tell you. And since you're his best friend, that indicates you have a great deal in common, share similar views, lifestyles, and—"

"Conjecture on the part of the witness. I'm being found guilty by association."

"You're being found guilty by the fact that you just kissed the socks off me, buster."

"Ah, but you kissed me back," he said, looking extremely pleased with himself.

"That's beside the point," Lisa mumbled.

"No, that *is* the point. Think about it. See you at seven," he said, turning and heading for the stairs.

Lisa opened her mouth to deliver a snappy retort, but for the life of her couldn't think of one thing to say. Cam sprinted across the sand, lifting his hand in a wave. She nodded slightly, a deep frown on her face as she watched him settle into the smooth, powerful run of a man who had total control of his body.

Yes, Lisa decided, Cam was a man in control, in charge. The aura of authoritativeness he had about him spoke volumes. Men probably moved out of his way without realizing they had done it. And women? The reverse would be true. They'd be pulled toward him by the magnetism of his masculinity, then held in place by those dark pirate eyes of his. He was dangerous, this Cam Porter. She herself had succumbed to that compelling gaze and that mind-boggling kiss.

She'd leaped into his arms without hesitation. Well, that was enough of that baloney. It wasn't going to happen again.

With a snort of disgust Lisa realized she was staying on the deck until she could no longer see Cam running along the beach. She spun around and went into the house, then on to the room housing her computer. The pirate and his maiden were due for an argument, and given Lisa's present mood, it was going to be a beaut. That little gal was about to tell the rogue where he could put himself.

"You too, Porter," she said under her breath. "I'm wise to you now."

Cam ran with an easily executed steady rhythm, the sand flying beneath his feet. Words slammed against his mind with the same cadence of his shoes on the beach, and a deep frown knitted his dark brows together.

He shouldn't have kissed Lisa Peterson. He'd known it was wrong before he'd done it, but he couldn't have stopped himself if someone had put a gun to his head. He had a love-'em-and-leave-'em attitude regarding women, just as Bret did. A temporary involvement with Lisa could very well jeopardize his long-standing friendship with Bret, and Cam didn't want that to happen.

But oh, man, she'd looked so feminine and enticing standing there in her skimpy shorts, her hair tousled, her big green eyes gazing up at him. So he'd kissed her. And what a kiss it had been. Desire had raced through him like a flash fire, and he'd wanted to make love to her right there on that chaise lounge.

"Hell," Cam grated, "she's Bret's little sister." No, damn it, she was a beautiful woman first, Bret's sister second. Lisa was old enough to make her own decisions regarding what she did. That was obvious. She'd walked out on Peterson Computer Corporation. Why had she done it? He'd come close to asking her on the deck, but he'd felt her tense up as if she was expecting him to grill her, so he'd dropped it.

A mysterious lady was Lisa Peterson, Cam mused, and a very desirable one. No, he was going to stay away from her. She was Bret's sister, and that fact wasn't going to disappear by his wishing it wasn't true. His sense of loyalty to his best friend included not seducing his younger sister. But Lisa had been heaven itself in his arms, her lips as sweet as warm honey. She'd molded to him as though she'd been custom-made for him. And he wanted her.

"You're a real sleazeball, Porter," he said, increasing the tempo of his run.

The telephone was ringing when Cam entered the house, and he snatched up the receiver.

"'Lo," he said, wiping his sweaty brow with his forearm.

"Been running?" a deep voice said. "You sound a bit winded."

"Ah, hell, Santini, don't you know what the word vacation means?" Cam said, his jaw tightening.

"Relax. I'm just keeping in touch, that's all. Wanted to thank you again for that little detour you made for us while you were where you were. Nice job, very smooth."

"Yeah, well, my own outfit had me dodging bullets. You guys got a knife pulled on me."

"You can handle yourself."

"The point is, Santini, I'm sick of it. I'm definitely through running errands for you, and I'm thinking about chucking the other, too."

"And do what? Work for Peterson Computer Corporation?"

"Been doing your homework, I see," Cam said, barely controlling his rising temper.

"We look after our own. I know you're tired, Cam. I'm delighted that you're taking this break. Not just because you're one of my agents, who might make a mistake if you're worn out. I'm concerned about you as a person, a human being. For my own peace of mind, I want to know you're fully rested before you work for me again."

"I said I'm through with your agency, Santini. If I come back at all, it will be only as a computer expert for the Feds."

"Come on, Cam. You thrive on the excitement working for us gives you. You'd be bored stiff being nothing more than straight civil service. As for Peterson Computer? Forget it. Your brain would stagnate. I can't picture you sitting behind a desk all day. Besides, the tempting half of the company copped out two years ago."

"Leave Lisa out of this, Santini," Cam grated.

"Lisa, is it? You're a fast worker," Santini said, chuckling. "Of course, you are staying with her brother, so I guess it makes sense that you'd have met her already. Don't get any fancy plans where Miss Peterson is concerned. She doesn't take kindly to men with secrets."

"What's that supposed to mean?" His grip on the phone receiver tightened.

"Your little trips here and there for us aren't public knowledge, my friend," Santini said.

"So? It's all done for this country."

"True. You're a very patriotic fella. It still doesn't erase the fact that you're not entirely what you appear to be on the surface. If you're serious—which I doubt—about ceasing operations with us, you'd have to be debriefed and go through channels."

"I know that. What's the point of this sermonette?" Cam demanded, impatient.

"Lisa Peterson is an extremely intelligent woman. If you get close to her, she's going to figure out you're hiding something by the questions you'll evade answering. As I said, she doesn't take kindly to men with secrets."

"Stuff it, Santini."

"You definitely need a vacation," Santini said, chuckling. "Enjoy yourself, Cam. See you soon."

"The hell you will," Cam said, slamming down the receiver. Yeah, okay, so he'd sounded genuinely concerned that Cam was bone weary, but Santini was still really strutting his stuff, letting Cam know they were watching him. What did they think he was going to do? Take out an ad in the newspaper announcing that he'd been an operative for the government on numerous occasions over the past ten years, in addition to his civil-service duties? Yeah, right. He'd go through the debriefing procedure and be finished with it once and for all. He'd had enough, had scars on his body to prove it, and was getting out while his mind was still in one piece.

Damn, he hated the idea that he was being hovered over like a naughty boy. If he'd known they were going to do that, he'd have never come to Bret's. He'd never have spoken to Lisa. They didn't deserve to have their lives poked into like this. Santini was right. Cam definitely needed a vacation.

Uttering a string of colorful expletives, Cam strode down the hall, and a few minutes later was standing in the shower, the hot water beating against his body.

Should he move to a hotel? he wondered. No, it was too late now. Santini and company had him covered, knew all about Lisa, Bret, and Peterson Computer. Operatives threatening to quit were potentially dangerous, he supposed. They could decide to sell what they knew to the highest bidder. There was no sense in asking to be debriefed now, because Santini would just stall, wait for Cam to change his mind. Both Santini and Cam's own boss had told Cam to take a month off, and now he had no choice but to do it. Wonderful.

But what had Santini meant by his veiled remarks about Lisa? Did it tie into her leaving Peterson Computer? How had secrets touched her life in the past? If some low-life had hurt her, he'd—

"Easy, Porter," Cam said, drying himself off with a fluffy towel. Where were these protective feelings toward Lisa coming from? Bret was there to take care of her. Then who was this unknown guy with secrets who had gotten to her somehow? So many questions, and he wanted some answers. And if Lisa wanted answers from him? Santini was right. Lisa was superintelligent. He'd have to be very careful, or she'd dump him on his butt. Whatever happened to staying away from her because she was Bret's sister?

"Think in circles much, Cameron?" he said to his reflection in the mirror. "Keep it up, and they'll drum you out on a Section Eight."

* * *

Just before seven, Lisa inspected her image in the full-length mirror in her bedroom and decided she looked extremely attractive. She ought to; this was the sixth outfit she'd had on. But at last her appearance met with her approval. Her white slacks hugged her in all the right places, and the green silk blouse was exactly the same shade as her eyes. A smile would help immensely, she thought, but she was too furious with herself to produce one.

Now, in addition to all her other flaky behavior with regard to Cameron Porter, she'd flitted around in a dither trying to decide what to wear for their evening out. She hadn't fussed this much when she'd had a date with the much-sought-after quarterback in high school. And tonight wasn't even a real date. It was Bret playing camp director, deciding who should pair up with whom.

"I swear, Lisa Peterson," she said to her reflected image, "you are extremely lacking in sophistication." Actually, she decided, her absurd behavior was Cam's fault. He had seemed to follow her around through the remaining hours of the afternoon, lurking in the shadows of her subconscious. There he'd be, smiling that hundred-watt smile, chuckling that sexy sound, and kissing her. That kiss had nearly melted her bones. He'd had no right to kiss her, but he'd done it, and therefore the jangled state of her nerves was entirely his fault. She liked that line of reasoning much better. When in doubt, plead not guilty and blame it all on the other guy.

Lisa laughed softly and went into the living room. Who was she trying to kid? She had responded to Cam's touch and kiss, and had enjoyed every minute of it. It had been a bit frightening to become so alive, so aware of her own femininity, while in his arms, but it had also been wonderful. When had she ever felt desire like that swirl within her? Potent stuff, that physical chemistry, when it got going. That's all it had been, of course, plain, old-fashioned lust, and she wasn't going back for a second helping. But while it had been taking place? Delicious.

A knock sounded at the door, and Lisa went to answer it, a genuine smile now on her face.

"Hello, Cam," she said after opening the door.

"Miss Peterson," he said, smiling as he stepped into the room. "For the second time today, I come as the official bearer of news."

"Oh? And what, pray tell, is your most current bulletin? Where's Bret?"

"That's my news. Suzanne has been called in at the last minute to substitute for another flight attendant. Suzanne is a flight attendant."

"Yes, I know."

"Anyway, Suzanne is pressed for time, so we're meeting them at the restaurant, then Bret will drive her straight to the airport."

"Oh, well, I—"

"Also," Cam went on, "I need to tell you that you look lovely, very beautiful. What the color of that blouse does to your eyes and my pulse rate should be against the law. I'd like to kiss you, but I won't, because you'd probably pop me in the chops. There. That's the seven o'clock news. Ready to go?"

Lisa blinked once, nodded, mumbled something about getting her purse and hurried into the bedroom. She took a deep, steadying breath and told herself she was doing fine. After all, when she'd opened the door to Cam she'd ignored the wild beating of her heart.

She'd also ignored the funny sensation in the pit of her stomach and the fact that Cam smelled like soap, a woodsy after-shave, and that aroma that was simply him.

It had been much more difficult to pay little attention to the way his gray sports coat stretched across his wide shoulders and how his black slacks hugged his muscled thighs. His burgundy shirt did marvelous things for his ebony hair and his dark tan.

The curly black hair peeking above the two open buttons on his shirt had appeared enticing, but she'd managed to scoot her gaze on past.

She was doing fine. Sort of.

"All set," she sang out, reentering the living room. "Cam?" she said, glancing around.

The sliding glass door leading to the deck was open, and Lisa crossed the room and peered out.

"Cam?"

"Yeah, I'm here. I couldn't resist seeing this in the moonlight. It's really something."

Lisa walked to his side to gaze out over the water. "Yes, it is," she said.

"The view of the ocean from a beach crowded with people is nothing like this," Cam said. "There's certainly none of this peace, tranquility. It's nice, it really is. But that's what vacations are for, aren't they? To relax, unwind, regroup," he said, turning to look at her.

"Not always. Some people want excitement, thrills, adventure, while they're free of their daily routines."

"I don't," he said quietly.

"No, I sense that. You're drawn to the peaceful-ness of this beach, the ocean, like metal slivers to a magnet."

"You're very perceptive," he said, frowning slight-ly.

"Sometimes I am. Other times I've been known to read people completely wrong, thought they were something entirely different from what they were."

The man with secrets in her past, Cam's mind whispered. "Well, you pegged me right," he said. "I just want to relax."

"Your job must be very demanding."

"Yeah, it is. We'd better go meet Bret and Su-zanne."

"All right."

"Ah, hell," he said, cupping her face in his hands, "I guess you're just going to have to pop me in the chops."

Oh, thank goodness, Lisa thought as he claimed her mouth with his. She'd been aching for this since he'd walked in the door.

The kiss was long, powerful, and sensations of de-sire flooded through Lisa the moment Cam's warm, seeking lips and tongue met hers. The kiss deepened and time stood still. What could have been seconds, minutes, or hours later, Cam lifted his head.

"We'd..." he started, then cleared his throat roughly, "...better go."

Lisa nodded, deciding there was not enough breath left in her body to speak, and they went into the liv-ing room, Cam locking the door to the deck behind them.

What was it about this woman? Cam asked himself as they left the house. He wanted her like no other woman he had ever known.

"Do you know where the restaurant is?" Lisa said as they drove away from the house. Hooray, she had a voice.

"Yeah."

"Okay," she said absently. Why had she kissed Cam again? When he'd kissed her, touched her, she had registered a sense of coming home, of being where she belonged. The fear had come with the thought that he *wouldn't* take her into his arms. She had needed, wanted, to be there. And she wanted Cameron Porter. But back to the question. Why Cam?

"Those books that you write," Cam said, bringing Lisa from her thoughts. "Are they always about pirates?"

"They have been, but I just had a powwow with my agent and my editor, and the next novel by Jasmine Peters will have a handsome cowboy as the hero and be set in the early west."

"Jasmine Peters?"

"That's my pseudonym, a concession I made to my parents regarding my writing."

"They don't approve?"

"It's not that exactly. They read every word in my books. It's the fact that I left Peterson Computer to write them. That part is difficult for them to understand."

No joke, Cam thought ruefully. He didn't understand it either, but the little voice in his head told him this was not the time to ask.

"You want to ask me why I walked away from Bret and Peterson Computer, don't you?" Lisa said.

Cam's head snapped around to look at her. He quickly redirected his attention to the heavy traffic.

"I admit I'm curious," he said, nodding. "Bret said you'd needed a change, and the tone of his voice indicated the subject was closed."

"I needed a change," she said quietly. "End of story."

"All right, Lisa," he said. "I won't push the issue. But if you ever want to talk about it, I'll listen."

"Thank you, Cam. So, what about you? You're a computer whiz for the government, dashing around to exciting foreign countries like a jet-setter. No wonder you're exhausted. It's all that wine, women, and song."

Cam chuckled. "Not quite," he said. "I fly over the fancy cities to reach some grungy outpost in the middle of nowhere. Or, worse yet, in the middle of a jungle. Some of those folks aren't too hospitable."

"You mean it's dangerous for you to be there?"

"Sometimes."

"Have you ever been hurt?"

"Once or twice. It's easier for me if I go in alone, but if I have a crew to watch over, it gets to be a hassle."

"Cam," she said, leaning slightly toward him, "are we talking about guns here, people shooting at people, being generally rude?"

He laughed. "That's about it," he said. "They're very rude, have no social graces at all."

"You've never been shot, have you?" she said, her voice rising.

"As you can see, I'm very much alive. Isn't that the restaurant up ahead?"

"Yes. Answer the question," she said, poking him in the arm with her finger.

"It's old news," he said, shaking his head. "It's not worth talking about."

"You were shot," she said, nodding decisively. "How dare the government put you in that kind of danger? You're not a soldier; you're a computer expert. As a taxpayer, I don't approve of this."

"Oh, okay," Cam said, laughing, "I'll tell them that Lisa Peterson said to knock it off."

"No wonder you need a peaceful vacation. Does Bret know all this?"

"What I can tell him. Some of it's classified."

"I know Bret hopes you'll stay on at Peterson Computer, Cam. He's wanted you to work with him for years."

"I realize that, but I need some time to unwind before I make any decisions about my future. Changing careers is a heavy-duty thing. But then, you know that from experience. I'll sort it through, figure out what's best for me. One part of it is crystal-clear already. And the rest? Well, we'll see."

Cam drove into the parking lot of the restaurant, and a few minutes later was escorting Lisa inside the building. She looked up at him from beneath her lashes, replaying in her mind what he had told her.

He'd been shot in some grungy jungle? That was terrible. Working with computers wasn't supposed to be dangerous. They were fun, nifty little machines. She didn't want Cam to go back to that job, put himself in harm's way. It suddenly mattered—mattered very much—that nothing happened to Cameron Porter.

Three

————

Cam," Lisa said quietly, looking up at him, "what did you mean when you said that one part of your plans for your future is crystal-clear?"

He'd said too much to her already, Cam thought. She was just so easy to talk to, listened as though she really cared, and he'd rattled on and on. And she was sharp, had picked up on what he'd said. Santini would pin him to the wall if he knew how much he'd spilled to Lisa. Nothing classified, but more than Cam would usually say on the subject, and Lisa hadn't missed one word of it. He didn't need a vacation; he needed a keeper!

"Cam?" Lisa said.

"What? Oh, I . . ."

"There you are," a voice said.

Saved by big brother, Cam thought ruefully. "Hey, Bret," he said, smiling, "I wondered where you were."

"Holding our table," he said, then gave Lisa a quick kiss on the cheek. "Howdy, Jasmine," he said. "I see you brought your own pirate with you tonight. You really do look like one of those swashbucklers, Cam."

"Oh, thanks," Cam said, chuckling. "What's next? I parallel-park my ship, sneak across the silver sands in the moonlight, kidnap Lisa, and sail away?"

Promise? Lisa asked silently.

"Oh, at least," Bret said, laughing. "Come on, Suzanne is waiting. We're going to have to eat and run, so that I can get her to the airport on time. You two can enjoy a leisurely evening, though."

Bret led the way through the crowded restaurant, which was decorated with a nautical theme. Large fishing nets hung on walls dotted with starfish, shells and driftwood. The waitresses were dressed in old-fashioned costumes like those worn in taverns in the days when tall ships sailed the seas.

"Perfect place for a pirate, wouldn't you say?" Cam said, close to Lisa's ear. "Fits my new image."

"Indeed it does," she said, smiling. It was as though they'd all read her mind. She'd already decided that Cam could have stepped from the pages of one of her books. Yes, a pirate; tall and strong, dark, and possessing the unspoken authority of a man who moved through life on the course he had chosen. Was Cam going to rechart the course of his life? Stay at Peterson Computer? If he did, what would it mean to her well-ordered existence?

"Here we are," Bret said. "We made it through the obstacle course. Suzanne, you know Lisa, of course, and this is Cam Porter."

Suzanne was a tall, attractive brunette who immediately smiled and extended her hand to Cam.

"Hello, Cam," she said, "please excuse my cute little uniform, but I'm about to do my 'coffee, tea or me' number."

Cam took Suzanne's hand, his gaze flicking over her shapely figure.

"You won't have many takers for coffee or tea," he said, flashing her a dazzling smile.

Oh, brother, Lisa thought, plunking herself down in a captain's chair.

"Hands off, Porter," Bret said good-naturedly. "The rules haven't changed from the old days. We stay clear of each other's turf."

"Well, that was before I became a pirate," Cam said, settling his tall frame into a chair. "We rogues have a different handbook. I'm going to read all of Lisa's novels so I can get this right."

"You haven't read them?" Suzanne said. "They're wonderful. I feel as though I've been transported to another time and place. My father has all my copies now. He's having such fun, says it reminds him of the days he'd go see Errol Flynn movies. I can hardly wait for the next Jasmine Peters novel. You are writing, aren't you, Lisa?"

"Every day," she said, smiling. "And thank you for the compliments."

"Well," Suzanne said, "you have a special gift, a way to offer people an escape for a few hours from the pressures of their lives. I wish people would discover books like yours instead of reaching for a bottle of booze or drugs."

"Interesting thought," Cam said, frowning slightly. "I'll definitely read Jasmine Peters and see what's going on."

"Oh, you must," Suzanne said. "Especially if you're in training to become a pirate." She cocked her head to one side and looked at Cam. "Yes, I think you'll do. You'll need one of those billowing white shirts, though."

"Hey, what about me?" Bret said. "I could swing from the mast or whatever."

"You, my darling," Suzanne said, before kissing him quickly on the lips, "look like a California beach boy. Buy a surfboard, and your image will be complete."

"My feelings are probably hurt," Bret said, "but I'm too hungry to care. Bring on the food."

The four were soon tackling succulent lobster, cottage fries, salads, and a crusty loaf of homemade bread. The conversation was lively and sprinkled generously with laughter. When the waitress appeared to take their dessert orders, Suzanne looked at her watch and announced she had to dash. Goodbyes were exchanged, and she and Bret hurried away. Lisa and Cam decided on cheesecake and coffee.

"Suzanne is good company," Cam said. "Bret has himself a winner there."

"Yes, she's fun, and very intelligent," Lisa said. "She has a master's degree in education."

"So why doesn't she teach?"

"She did for a few years but decided it wasn't for her."

"Chucked her education to play waitress in the sky, huh?" Cam said, his jaw tightening slightly.

Lisa looked up at him quickly. "She didn't 'chuck' her education," she said. "No one can take what she's learned away from her. She simply got in touch with herself and found her place."

"Well, it's none of my business," he said, lifting a shoulder in a shrug. "Is Bret serious about her?"

"Bret isn't serious about anyone. I don't think he'll ever settle down, marry, have a family. Suzanne is just one of many in his little black book. Suzanne realizes that, and they get along just fine. I find no fault with the way Bret conducts his life. He's honest and upfront, makes no promises he doesn't intend to keep."

"Honest," Cam repeated.

"Yes, Bret is exactly who he presents himself to be. He treats his women with respect and dignity, and they enjoy his company. No one gets hurt."

"You seem to place a great deal of importance on honesty," Cam said. "You know, all-the-facts-on-the-table type of thing."

"Yes," she said quietly, "I do."

"No surprises."

"No deceit, Cam. There's a tremendous difference between the two."

Cam covered her hand with his on the top of the table. "Who hurt you, Lisa?" he said, looking directly into her eyes. "I saw it, the flicker of pain in your eyes when you spoke of deceit. Who was he?"

"To use your phrase, it's old news," she said, attempting a smile, and failing.

"Is it?" he said, his voice low. "Not if what he did to you is causing you to stay behind protective walls."

"I'm not," she said, attempting to pull her hand free.

Cam tightened his hold. "Aren't you?" he said, his gaze locked onto hers.

"Cheesecake and coffee," the waitress said. "Excuse me, folks."

Cam released Lisa's hand and leaned back to allow the waitress to place the dessert on the table.

Lisa fumed, straightening her napkin on her lap. Why wouldn't Cam just leave it alone, leave *her* alone? She had no intention of baring her soul to him, telling him of her naive stupidity in trusting, believing, loving Jim Weber. Jim Weber. Lord, that hadn't even been his real name.

"I'm sorry," Cam said after the waitress moved away. "I shouldn't have pushed you. I've obviously raked up some painful memories, and I had no right to do that. It's just that I feel as though I'm fighting ghosts, and that's tough to do. I want to get to know you better, Lisa, as corny as that line sounds. But," he added with a smile, "we pirates are persistent. We don't let a wall beat us. I'll either go over, around, or through it. I'd prefer to demolish it altogether."

"Why?" she said, frowning. "Why are you so intent on getting to know me better, as you so quaintly put it? Surely your male ego isn't so enormous you have to conquer every woman who crosses your path."

"Why do you suppose they call this cheesecake, when it's actually pie?"

"What?"

"It's made in a pie pan, sliced like a piece of pie, so why not label it cheese pie?"

"I take it we're changing the subject," Lisa said, her frown deepening.

"Yep," he said, shoveling cheesecake into his mouth.

"You certainly like to run this show, Mr. Porter," she said, stabbing at her dessert with her fork.

"Nope."

"Ha!"

Cam chuckled, the low, rumbling sound having its usual disconcerting effect on Lisa's pulse rate. She shot him another stormy glare, then concentrated on her dessert.

Well, Cam thought, he'd wriggled out of that one. Why did he want to get to know Lisa Peterson better? He couldn't respond to the question because he didn't know the answer! Yeah, okay, he wanted her. Physically desired her, ached with the need to make love with her. But it was more than that. Emotions were interwoven with his lust. A strange protectiveness, possessiveness, toward Lisa kept assaulting him. An urgent need to erase all pain from the depths of her incredible green eyes and see only happiness there.

He was treading in dangerous waters. He knew it, and didn't care. His own life was so screwed up at the moment, he had no room for anything but the decisions he had to make regarding his future. But he was drawn to Lisa like a moth to a flame, and he couldn't seem to stop himself. What he was going to do about it, he didn't know. He sure didn't know a heck of a lot. Except for the fact that he wasn't walking away from Lisa Peterson. That part was very clear.

"Cam," Lisa said, bringing him from his rambling thoughts, "may I ask you something?"

"Sure," he said, smiling, "you can ask me anything you wish."

"But you might not answer."

He shrugged. "What's the question?"

"Is it my imagination, or do you highly resent those who have chosen not to pursue the career they studied for in college?"

Cam lifted his cup, took a swallow of coffee, then slowly replaced the cup on the saucer.

"'Highly resent' is a bit heavy," he said finally, looking at her. "It just seems like a terrible waste, that's all. Not everyone is able to go to college. They see their hopes and dreams stay just beyond their reach because they weren't able to go after the education they needed to attain them. People who have degrees and treat them as some insignificant detail in their lives, nothing of particular importance... Well, I don't quite understand where they're coming from."

"You mean people like me and Suzanne?"

"Look, Lisa, this conversation is going to lead to an argument between us. I think we'd better just drop it."

"But why do you feel so strongly about it? Everyone has the right to make choices. You obviously chose to stay in the field that you majored in in college, but that doesn't mean that all people—"

"No, I didn't," Cam interrupted her.

"You didn't major in computer science?"

"I didn't go to college," he said, reaching for his cup again.

"You didn't go to...but Bret said you're one of the finest computer experts he's ever known. You have a high-ranking job with the government. How did you learn so much without formal training?"

"High school, then the army. I enlisted with the idea of going to college later on the GI Bill. It just didn't work out that way."

"Why not?"

"My parents were killed right after I joined the army and I . . . Lisa, this is a very boring story."

"No, it isn't," she said, placing her hand on his forearm. "Do you mind talking about it?"

"It's not that interesting. I had two younger sisters who went to live with our grandparents. That part was all right, because it got them out of the stinking neighborhood we'd grown up in in L.A. Thing was, our grandparents were retired and living on a fixed income. It was up to me to send money for my sisters' support. College for me was a forgotten dream. Bret and I were assigned to computers in the army, and I took a couple of correspondence courses at the same time. After our hitch, Bret went to Stanford. I went civil service."

"I see," Lisa said, nodding thoughtfully.

And then Santini, Cam thought. One of Santini's men had gotten jumped in an alley by three guys in a hell-hole overseas, and Cam had waded in and saved the joker's butt. Santini had checked Cam out and offered him big bucks just to follow orders. Cam had jumped at the chance to have more money to send home. Thing was, when his sisters were both married and the grandparents had died of old age, Cam hadn't quit. One more assignment, then one more, then . . .

"Where are your sisters now?" Lisa asked.

"Oh, they're happily married, have kids. One is in Nevada, the other in Michigan. My grandparents died several years ago."

"Did you take the overseas assignments, the dangerous ones, because they offered the extra hazardous-duty pay you needed for your family?"

Cam shifted in his chair. "Yeah," he said. "Hey, I told you this was a boring story. Eat your pie, or cake, or whatever it is."

"But why did you stay in those types of situations once your sisters were married?"

"It didn't seem all that bad," he said, shrugging. "I grew up fighting in the streets, knew how to take care of myself. Lately, though, I... Damn it, what is it about you? I'm not in the habit of giving dissertations on the life and times of Cameron Porter. You get me started, and I don't shut up."

"I'm honored that you feel comfortable enough to share with me, Cam," she said, smiling at him warmly.

"And you, Lisa?" he said, frowning. "When do you lower some of those walls around yourself and give me a glimpse of who you are? Why did you leave Peterson Computer? Who hurt you in the past? Are the two things connected? You're a top-notch computer programmer with a degree from MIT, and you write romance novels. Why? What happened to you in the real world that caused you to escape to one of fantasy?"

"That's enough, Cam," she said, green eyes flashing with anger.

"Oh, really? You seem to think it's perfectly acceptable to dig out all the little tidbits about me, so why shouldn't I expect the same in return? I want answers, Lisa," he said, a muscle jumping along his jaw.

"Well, you're not going to get them," she said, getting to her feet. "I would appreciate it if you'd take me home. I'll wait for you in the lobby," she said, then walked briskly away.

Cam muttered an oath as he signaled to the waitress. Now Lisa was all in a snit. But he had a legitimate point. Sharing wasn't one-sided. He'd practically told her his life history, then she got bent out of shape when he pushed her for more information about *her*. And she said *he* liked to run the show?

"Your bill, sir," the waitress said. "You pay the cashier in the lobby."

"Thanks," he said, getting to his feet.

"Do come again," she said, smiling provocatively at him.

"You bet," he said, leaving a generous tip on the table. "See you around."

"I hope so."

Cam shook his head as he made his way through the clusters of tables. There were always plenty of women available, he mused. Ready, willing and able. Then why was he messing around with Lisa Peterson, who was holding him at arm's length and had a fiery temper and more secrets than the Pentagon? He didn't need this! But he had a knot in his stomach that told him he had to do everything in his power to smooth her ruffled feathers.

The lobby was crowded. Cam quickly paid the bill, then searched for Lisa. He saw her in profile, standing with her arms crossed over her breasts, staring at the seascape on the wall. His gaze swept over her, missing not the slightest detail of her exquisite figure: the lush breasts, the gentle slope of her hips, the tight roundness of her buttocks. Her legs, he knew, were shapely and tanned, inviting his fingers to skim along their satiny length.

Cam's scrutiny was thorough, causing his blood to pound in his veins as he looked at her. His dark eyes played over her delicate features. Even though her face was partially hidden from his view, he could see her clearly in his mind's eye. Those great big emerald eyes of Lisa's were enough to turn a man inside out. They could sparkle with merriment, flash like laser beams when she was angry, and turn smoky like rich jade when they spoke of her inner desires. Her hair was a silken mass of blond-and-gold curls. Strawberry blond was the official name for the color, he supposed, and it was lovely.

Hell, he even liked her pert little nose and her stubborn Peterson chin.

Lisa was something, all right, Cam decided. But *he* was supposed to be the pirate around there. Then why did he have this sneaking suspicion that Lisa was in the process of capturing his heart? And with it his soul, mind and body.

Cam shoved his hands into his pockets and walked slowly to Lisa's side.

"Ready to go?" he said quietly.

"Yes," she said, not looking at him.

The drive back to Lisa's was made in total silence. She sat with her hands clutched tightly in her lap, staring out the side window. Cam glanced at her often, but made no attempt to break the silence, nor to sever the crackling web of tension in the car. When they reached her house, he turned off the ignition.

Lisa took a steadying breath. "Cam," she said, her voice hushed, "I'm sorry for the way I behaved. I did keep after you to tell me about yourself, then refused to share things about my own life. That wasn't fair, and I apologize."

"Let's go inside," he said.

"No, I—"

"Inside," he said, getting out of the car.

In the living room, Lisa turned to Cam where they stood just inside the door.

"I think it would be best," she said, "if you went on to Bret's now."

"Yes, thank you," he said, looking at her steadily, "I *would* like a nightcap. Do you have any brandy?"

"No."

"Where do you keep it?"

She swore. "In the kitchen," she said, planting her hands on her hips.

"I'll get it. Make yourself comfortable."

"This is my house!"

"And it's a nice place," he said, heading for the kitchen. "I like the way you've decorated it. I'll meet you on the deck. I have to check something out."

Cocky and arrogant, Lisa fumed silently. Arrogant and cocky. Cameron Porter was infuriating. And look at this. Her dumb feet were moving her right toward the deck like a good little soldier following orders from the big man.

"For Pete's sake," she said, flinging the door open and stepping out onto the deck.

Cam appeared a few moments later, handed her a brandy snifter, then crossed the deck to lean his elbows on the railing and stare out over the quiet expanse.

"I'll be damned," he said.

Don't ask, Lisa told herself. She didn't care what he was checking out and found so all-fired fascinating. This man was not going to push her buttons. Oh, damn. "What is it?" she said.

"Come here a second."

Lisa gritted her teeth and moved to the railing, keeping a two-foot distance between her and Cam.

"Well?" she said.

"Look," he said, gesturing with the snifter. "Silver sands, just like I said. The moon and stars are transforming the beach into silver sands. That is one beautiful sight. I can really picture a ship out there with tall masts and a crow's nest. And here comes the pirate to claim his maiden. He's wearing his bed-sheet shirt, of course."

"Of course," Lisa said, smiling in spite of herself.

Cam shifted to face her, and she stared at him wide-eyed, her heart racing. The almost eerie luminescence from the heavenly spectacle cast flickering shadows and silvery hues over Cam, making him seem even bigger, darker, more powerful. He set his snifter on the railing and advanced slowly toward her. Lisa forgot to breathe. She was pinned in place by the fathomless depths of Cam's dark eyes, her knees were trembling, and she was *not* breathing. Cam took her snifter from her lifeless fingers, set it on the railing, then cradled her face in his large hands. He said one word in a voice so low, so seductive, so incredibly male, that she was sure her bones were dissolving.

"Lisa."

"Oh, dear heaven," she whispered, then lifted her arms to circle his neck.

Cam moved one hand to the nape of her neck, the other to the small of her back, then pulled her up against him, his mouth sweeping down over hers. She molded her soft curves to his rugged contours and returned the kiss in total abandon. Cam's tongue dueled with hers in a rhythmic dance in the darkness of her mouth, filling her senses with a shattering pleasure that brought a purr from her throat. A shimmer of heat coursed through her, then burst into a raging flame of desire.

"Cam," she gasped.

"Ah, Lisa," he said, his voice gritty. He drew a ragged breath, then claimed her mouth again, plunging his tongue deep within.

Cam's hands moved to Lisa's back, roaming over the rich silk of her blouse, then inching forward to the sides of her breasts. Her body pressed to his was sweet torture, a promise of ecstasy. Her feminine aroma ignited his passion even further, causing a shudder to ripple through his massive body. How he wanted her.

Cam strove for control, fighting against the coiling, burning need within him. Never had he been consumed by such desire. He groaned deep in his chest as he ravished her mouth in urgent, frenzied motions. His mind warred with his body. Missives beat against his brain with the same pulsing cadence of the blood pounding in his veins. He pulled himself painfully back from the hazy mist of passion that had held him in an iron grip, then jerked his lips from Lisa's.

"No," he grated, grasping her upper arms and setting her away from him.

"Cam?" she said, stumbling slightly as he released her.

He turned to the railing and gripped it with such force that his knuckles went white from the pressure. His labored breathing echoed in the quiet night.

Lisa pressed trembling fingers to her kiss-swollen lips and stared at Cam, seeing the rigid set to his shoulders, his tight hold on the railing. The tension emanating from him seemed to beat against her with a painful intensity.

What had she done? her mind questioned frantically. Never before had she responded to a man's kiss as she had to Cam's. She had not wanted to end the kiss, nor to leave the safe, strong haven of his arms. And she had wanted, needed even more. Cam. All of him. She wanted the feel of his hands and lips on her aching breasts. Every inch of her was crying out to be touched by Cameron Porter. She wanted him to make love to her, totally, completely, to fill her with his masculinity.

"No," she whispered.

"I know," Cam said, a weary quality to his voice as he turned to look at her. "I know. Too soon, too fast, all the usual clichés. They're true, and they apply, make sense, the whole nine yards. And I don't give a damn. I want you, Lisa, like I have never wanted a woman before in my life. And you want me. Sounds simple enough: two adults who desire each other."

"Cam, I—"

"But it isn't simple," he said, raking his hand through his hair, a muscle throbbing in the strong column of his neck, "because there are emotions coming into play here, things I don't understand, nor particularly welcome. What in the hell are you doing to me, Lisa Peterson?"

"Me? Me! You're the one riding roughshod over my mind, my body, my common sense. I don't go around adhering myself to men's bodies, dissolving into a lump of jelly when I'm held and kissed. No, this isn't simple. It's complicated, frightening. You arrive from God knows where and turn my life into a jumbled mess. I have the urge to tell you to take a hike across your silver sands and not come back, and...and in the next breath I don't want you to leave me. Oh, damn you, Cameron.''

Cam reached out one long arm and closed his fingers around her hand, pulling her to him.

"No," she said.

"Shh," he said, gathering her close to his chest and enclosing her in the strong circle of his arms.

Lisa sighed in defeat and rested her head on his chest, relishing his aroma and his strength, the heat of his body. He held her close, his chin on top of her head, the only sound in the silvery night being the gentle lapping of the waves on the shore. Minutes ticked away, and neither spoke or moved.

"What would a pirate do in a situation like this?" Cam said finally.

"Are you kidding? He'd have jumped my bones by now."

Cam chuckled, causing Lisa's head to bounce on his chest. "Lord knows my body was willing," he said. "It was my mind that got in the way. Some pirate trainee I am."

Lisa tilted her head back to smile up at him. "You've settled on your career plans? You're going to be a pirate?"

"Yep," he said, returning her smile. "I'll read all of Jasmine Peters's books, and find out the nitty-gritty of what it takes to be a ravishing pirate. Do those guys have a group medical plan? Paid vacations? What are the perks?"

"You're crazy," she said, laughing.

"And you," he said, very serious again, "are beautiful. You scare the hell out of me, Lisa Peterson. I'd better leave now. I'm not going to kiss you again tonight, Lisa. I'm hanging on by a thread as it is. I'll talk to you tomorrow.''

"All right."

"I'll let myself out. Good night," he said, and kissed her on the forehead.

"Night, Cam," she said, her voice hardly more than a whisper.

Lisa wrapped her hands around her elbows and stared out over the silver sands of the beach until she could no longer hear the sound of Cam's car as he drove away. She sighed, then picked up the brandy snifters.

"What am I going to do?" she said to the umbrella of stars overhead. "What am I going to do about Cam?"

With another wobbly sigh and a shake of her head, she walked slowly into the house.

When Cam entered the living room of Bret's house, his host pushed himself to his feet.

"Cam," Bret said, nodding slightly, a frown on his face.

"Hello, Bret," Cam said, shrugging out of his jacket. "Suzanne make her flight on time?"

"Yeah."

"Seeing you with her made me realize that my staying here could cramp your style. It might be better if I moved to a hotel."

"No need. Unless, of course, you think my knowing what time you get in will cramp *your* style under the circumstances."

"What circumstances, Bret?"

"You tell me."

"Lisa's a big girl now, Bret, all grown up."

"Damn it, Porter," he roared. "She's my sister."

"Second behind being a woman," Cam shot back. "She can make her own decisions."

"Did you take her to bed?" Bret said, his jaw tight. "Is that where you've been all this time?"

"That's none of your damn business, Peterson!"

"The hell it isn't. If you hurt Lisa, Cam, I swear I'll take you apart."

Cam snorted in disgust. "You and what army? I learned to fight dirty on the streets, remember? Oh, you're big, but I'm bigger, and you don't have the survival instincts I do. I'd whip your butt, and you know it."

"Damn you," Bret said, starting toward Cam.

In a blur of motion, Cam moved with the power of a sleek cat. In the next instant, Bret was slammed against the wall, his shirt held in Cam's steel grip.

"Now, you listen to me," Cam said, his voice low and menacing, "and get it right the first time. *I did not sleep with your sister!* That tiny whisper of a woman has me so tied up in knots I've got an ache in my gut. I could have made love to her, Peterson, but I didn't. Know why? Because what she's doing to my body, she's also doing to my mind!"

"No kidding?" Bret said, a smile tugging at his lips.

"It's not funny!" Cam bellowed. "She's turning my brain into scrambled eggs, and my body is begging for mercy. I walked away from the most desirable woman I've ever met, and I have no idea why. I should be with her right now, instead of talking to her harebrained brother. Lisa doesn't need protecting. *I* do!" Cam let go of Bret and stepped back.

"I'll be damned," Bret said, a wide grin on his face now. "I've never seen you like this, old buddy," Bret said, whomping Cam on the back. "You're really jangled. Want a drink?"

"No."

"Seriously, Cam, I don't want to see Lisa hurt. Not again."

Cam's head snapped up. "Who was he, Bret?" he said. "I tried to get her to talk about it, but she shut me out."

"If she wants you to know, she'll tell you. Look, I realize I was out of line. Lisa is a grown woman, and she'd throw a fit if she knew I was hovering around like a baby-sitter. It's just that you and I don't exactly sign up for long-term commitments with women. I guess you've figured out, though, that Lisa is special."

"Yeah."

"And?"

"And what?" Cam said, frowning. "You explain it to me, Bret. Tell me what these weird emotions are I'm registering. Protectiveness? Possessiveness? Me? No thanks, I'll pass. But I'd hate to be the next poor joker I see looking at her too long. Bret, I think I'm in trouble."

"Cam, I *know* you're in trouble."

"I have no intention of falling in love with Lisa Peterson," Cam said, none too quietly.

"Your objection to the situation is duly noted, Mr. Porter," Bret said, pointing a finger in the air.

"Knock it off."

"Thing is," Bret said, staring into space, "how does one stop falling in love once one has begun? Protectiveness? Possessiveness? I do believe you're on the road already."

"Bull."

"Well, have you ever felt those things toward a woman before?" Bret said, raising his eyebrows.

"No."

"I haven't either. I repeat my statement. You're definitely in trouble. I sure don't have any advice for you. You're playing out of my league, chum. I have never been, nor do I intend to be, in love."

"We don't know that I'm in love," Cam said. "This is an insane conversation."

"You're right. Let's get some sleep. Maybe things will be clearer in the morning."

"I'm too wired to sleep. I'm going for a run."

"Suit yourself. You're still coming to Peterson Computer tomorrow, aren't you?"

"Yeah," Cam said, nodding, "I'm eager to see this spiffy new building of yours."

"It's a beauty. The whole operation is top-notch. Cam?"

"Yeah?"

"I saw you in more than one fight when we were in the army, and I was awed by your reflexes, the way you moved, handled yourself. But that was nothing compared to now. You've been doing more than straight civil-service stuff for the Feds, haven't you?"

Cam stiffened, then took a deep breath, staring up at the ceiling for a long moment before looking at Bret again.

"Never mind," Bret said quietly. "You answered my question without saying a word. Please, Cam, don't hurt Lisa."

Bret turned and walked slowly from the room, his hands deep in his pockets.

Cam swore under his breath.

Four

Lisa slid the disk into its cardboard jacket, and got to her feet. She pressed her fists into the small of her back, then rotated back and forth in an attempt to loosen muscles cramped from many hours in front of the computer.

She was extremely pleased with her day's work, and had accomplished far more than she'd planned in connection with her self-imposed schedule. She was also pleased that she had pushed the thought of Cam Porter to the recesses of her mind and not allowed him to intrude on her mental space.

Until now.

Now, there he was, front row center, dancing before her eyes in all his magnificent glory. He appeared so real that Lisa felt as though she could reach out and touch him; feel those steely muscles under her fingertips, sift the night darkness of his hair through her hands, savor the sensation of his lips on hers, and inhale his special aroma.

"Darn it," Lisa said as desire licked through her.

It was one of those times, Lisa decided, when she needed to be with people, needed to forget the characters in her book. And forget Cameron Porter! People read her books to escape. Well, the writer had to escape from the book.

With a decisive nod, Lisa entered the living room and picked up the telephone receiver. A short time later she was headed for the bedroom, having made plans with her friend Tracey to meet for dinner. She hummed softly under her breath and decided she was in a terrific mood, in spite of her grueling day. And in spite of Cam, who had the audacity to follow her right into the shower.

Three hours later, Lisa unlocked the door and walked slowly into the living room. She sank onto the sofa with a sigh, a deep frown on her face.

The evening had been a disaster. She had been unable to keep her attention centered on Tracey's non-stop chatter and had, instead, found herself scrutinizing every tall, dark man who came into the restaurant. But none was quite as tall as Cam or had shoulders quite as wide, a tan as bronze, features as ruggedly handsome. None had been Cam Porter. And Lisa missed him.

She wanted him there, now, with her.

She wanted him to pull her into his arms and kiss her senseless.

And she wanted him to make love with her.

"What an unthinkable thought," Lisa said to the empty room. "Shame on you, Lisa Peterson."

With a snort of disgust, Lisa got to her feet and wandered down the hall to the computer room. She flipped on the light, and saw the perforated paper in the basket where it had fallen after coming from the printer. She tore it off and read the message.

HOW CAN A PIRATE RAVISH A MAIDEN IF SAID RAVISHEE ISN'T HOME? YOU'RE PUTTING MY TRAINING BEHIND SCHEDULE. PLANT YOUR CUTE BEHIND AND FLY THOSE NIMBLE FINGERS OVER THE KEYS. THIS PIRATE NEEDS TO KNOW YOU ARE A-OK. CAM.

"I wonder when he sent this," Lisa said, smiling.

She sat down, entered the proper code, and began to type.

HELLO, SIR PIRATE. THE MAIDEN HAS RETURNED.

The reply came on the screen almost instantly.

IT'S ABOUT TIME. I THINK I'M PERMANENTLY ATTACHED TO THIS CHAIR. HOW'S THIS FOR SUBTLE? WHERE IN THE HELL HAVE YOU BEEN?

Arrogant and rude again, Lisa thought, laughing softly. It was none of Cam's business where she'd been. But did his less-than-polite query mean that he cared about who she'd been with?

HAD DINNER WITH A GIRLFRIEND, she typed. PLEASANT OUTING, BUT NOT EARTH-SHATTERING. NOW I THINK I'LL GO WIGGLE MY TOES IN THE SILVER SANDS.

The white letters of Cam's reply danced across the screen.

WOULD YOUR TOES LIKE COMPANY?

Yes, Lisa's mind whispered. Oh, yes, Cam. It hadn't been a day since she'd seen him; it had been an eternity. But she'd type in something light, humorous, casual, ultrasophisticated, to invite him to come.

YES, was all her trembling fingers managed to accomplish.

ON MY WAY. OVER AND OUT OR WHATEVER.

Lisa jumped to her feet and hurried into the bedroom to change into jeans and a lightweight sweater and freshen her makeup. Cam was on his way, her heart sang.

Cam stripped off his faded T-shirt and pulled on a navy-blue sweater. He stepped into the bathroom to comb his thick hair in front of the mirror, and jerked in surprise when his reflection smiled back at him.

Look at that, he fumed. He'd had that foolish grin on his face all this time and hadn't even known it. He was really losing it. There he'd sat, slouched in that chair in front of the computer, waiting for Lisa to get home. Bret had gone out hours before, mumbling something about seeing Cam at breakfast.

Cam had wandered aimlessly around the house, unable to concentrate on anything but Lisa. Somewhere in the middle of the day he'd resolved to stay away from one Miss Lisa Peterson. So much for that plan. Admitting defeat, he'd activated the computer, feeling a surge of anticipation as he sent the signal that he wished to converse with her through the machines. But she hadn't been home. So he'd printed out his message and waited.

Like a teenager with a crush, he'd waited.

Like a complete idiot, he'd waited, sitting there like a dunce for hours.

Or had he waited like a man in love?

"Well?" he said, leaning closer to the mirror. "Answer that one, Porter. Don't know, huh? Oh, the hell with it."

Cam spun on his heel and left the room. A few minutes later he was driving, well above the speed limit, to Lisa's.

Lisa filled her lungs with the moist, salty night air, which was slightly chilly. The sand beneath her bare feet was damp but still fairly warm from its daylong bath of sunshine. She wiggled her toes, then lifted her face to gaze at the star-studded sky, which twinkled a million hellos in silvery splendor.

A shiver of excitement feathered along her spine as she heard Cam's car approach, then stop, the door slamming a moment later. She didn't move. She stood facing the ocean, her hands wrapped loosely around her elbows, and waited. For Cam.

She could picture him so clearly as he strode toward her. He was probably dressed in jeans, snug, faded jeans, and a sweater to ward off the chill. His dark hair would be combed over his ears and taper along his neck, just beginning to hint that he needed a trim. His ebony eyes would miss no detail of her, the silver sands, or the heavenly greeting of the moon and stars.

Any moment now, any breathless, heart-stopping moment, Cam would be there.

And he was.

Cam placed his large hands on Lisa's shoulders and gently turned her to face him. Their gaze met, held; their heartbeats quickened. A wondrous trembling began deep within Lisa as Cam slowly lowered his lips to hers. A soft sigh escaped her throat as he gathered her to his chest, and she stood on tiptoe to wrap her arms around his neck.

The kiss intensified. Tongues met, flickered, dueled, danced with each other, first in her mouth, then in his. Desire ripped through Cam with a sweet pain as he savored Lisa's taste and aroma. She nestled against him; soft curves to rugged contours, feminine warmth to masculine heat, woman to man.

Cam's manhood pressed hard against Lisa as he tightened his hold on her, crushing her breasts to his chest. He lifted his head a fraction of an inch to draw a ragged breath, then claimed her mouth once again, his questing tongue finding hers. Her breasts grew heavy, aching for his touch, and she trembled in his arms, clinging to him for support.

"Ah, Lisa," Cam said, his voice so vibrant with passion that she nearly went limp in his arms.

He wove his fingers through her silky curls and pressed her head to his chest, his thundering heart echoing her own. She wrapped her arms around his waist and splayed her hands on his back, feeling the corded muscles beneath his sweater. Her senses were filled with the taste, the scent, the essence of Cam.

With a sigh he moved her gently away from him, trailing his thumb over her smooth cheek as she gazed up at him.

"Hello, Lisa Peterson," he said, smiling slightly.

"Hello, Cam Porter," she said, hearing the thread of breathlessness in her own voice.

"I missed you today."

"Yes."

"This isn't just lust. You know that, don't you? Something else is happening between us, Lisa."

"I know."

"Here, on this beach, on these silver sands in the moonlight, it's as though we're the only two people in the universe. I want to make love with you in the glow of the stars and forget everything but you and the moment. But it's not that simple. There *is* a world out there pulling at us, and we don't match up very well. I don't even know where I'll be a month from now."

"Did you go to Peterson Computer with Bret?"

"Let's sit on the deck," he said, circling her shoulders with his arm. "Yeah, I went to Peterson Computer," he went on as they walked up the stairs. "I was very impressed."

Cam stopped speaking as they moved up the stairs and got settled in the padded chairs.

"Bret has done incredible things with that company," he continued. "You did, too, while you were there. The potential is mind-boggling."

"The work is very challenging," Lisa said, looking at him intently. "No two projects are the same."

"I realize that, but . . . I don't know, Lisa. I'm not accustomed to being cooped up in an office all day. I've always worked outside, had room to move around. Granted, I wasn't always in the plush spots of the world, but I wasn't sitting behind a desk. Bret is offering me a fantastic career opportunity, but I'm not positive that I have the temperament to handle it."

"You'd rather be shot at?"

Cam chuckled. "Of course not. And that doesn't always happen. I was hot under the collar over my last assignment, because we were guaranteed it was a safe area. Because of that, I took an entire crew in, then all hell broke loose. I realize now that it wasn't anyone's fault. I got everyone out alive, but I was in no mood to listen to the explanations as to what had gone wrong."

"I understand," Lisa said, nodding.

"I have to sort it all through, don't you see? I can't give Bret an answer until I'm sure I'm the right man for Peterson Computer. I'm walking around in a maze trying to find the proper path to take. I don't want anyone to be hurt by the decisions I make."

"Of course you don't."

"Lisa, the timing for us, of you and me, is really lousy. I'm feeling things for you that I've never experienced before, yet I'm in no position to pursue those new emotions, discover what they're all about, because you could very well be hurt in the process. I tell myself to leave you alone, not come near you again, then I fall all over my feet to get to you. I think I would have gone out of my mind if I hadn't been able to see you tonight. I'm not in terrific shape here."

"Cam, I really do understand. Leaving Peterson Computer was one of the most difficult decisions I've ever made. You're talking about your entire future."

"And I'm also talking about us," he said, taking her hand in his. "I don't want to hurt you, but I could. You know that something special is happening between us. What if I walk out of your life in a few weeks? What then?"

"I couldn't stop you, Cam," she said quietly.

"The decent thing would be for me to leave you alone starting right now. I sure wish I knew how I'm going to manage to do that. Lisa, demand I leave you alone, then buy a huge guard dog."

"No," she said, smiling. "Those grouchy dogs scare me to death."

"Do *I*?" he asked, his voice low. "Do I frighten you?"

"You? As a man, a person? No. The strange feelings within me, the way I respond to your kiss and touch? Yes. As long as I'm being so candid, I might as well tell you that I want to make love with you, and I've never been so brazen about it before in my life. I do want you, Cam."

"My libido can't take much more of this," he said with a groan. "I'm already coming apart at the seams. But, damn it, there *are* emotions intertwined here. No! No, we are not going to make love. We're not going to bed together. We're not going to share in what would be the most glorious union between...two people...who have ever...ah, hell!"

"I guess I shouldn't have said that."

"I know you want me as much as I want you. I'm the guy who's kissing you, remember?"

"I definitely remember," Lisa said, a rather wistful tone to her voice. "Maybe we should talk about something else."

"Yeah, I—" Cam started, then stiffened in his chair. "What in the— Infrared. Damn him!"

Lisa's eyes widened, and she gasped as Cam suddenly lunged to his feet and crossed the deck. In a smooth, tight, powerful motion he braced himself on the railing and vaulted over, taking off at a dead run the moment his feet hit the sand below.

"Cam!" she said, running to the railing and scanning the beach.

Lisa scrambled down the stairs, then stopped, seeing no sign of Cam. Her heart beat wildly against her ribs, and she was aware of the metallic taste of fear in her mouth.

Dear heaven, what was going on? her mind screamed. Infrared? A camera? Cam had said "Damn him." Who was out there, and what did he want with Cam? What was Cam doing now? She'd never seen anyone move so quickly, so automatically, and with such control. Bret kept himself in good shape, but Cam's actions had been different somehow. Frightened, she thought, Where was Cam?

A cold fury pumped through Cam as he ran along the beach, closing the distance between him and the shadowy figure within his view. A rage like nothing he had ever experienced pounded against his brain, causing a rushing noise in his ears. A few more yards and he'd have him!

Cam lunged through the air and tackled the fleeing man, bringing him down with a resounding thud. A hot pain shot through Cam's right forearm, but he ignored it as he flipped the man over and straddled him, gripping his throat.

"You're strangling me," the man gasped.

"Who sent you? Give me a name," Cam said, jaws clenched.

"No one. I'm taking pictures for a book I'm— Ugh!" he said as Cam's fingers tightened.

"With or without pain—make up your mind," Cam said, his voice low and menacing. "Makes no difference to me."

"You're killing me, Porter," the man rasped.

Cam reached over with his free hand and yanked the film from the camera.

"A name," Cam said again. "You're going back empty-handed, so you're already in trouble. The man doesn't like screw-ups."

"You know who it is. Give me a break. He'll have my butt."

"Humor me," Cam said, his voice harsh. "Let me hear it."

"Damn it! It's Santini, and he's sticking to you like superglue, Porter. You're making him nervous."

"Do tell," Cam said dryly.

"There's blood on my neck! I can feel it. I told you you were killing me."

"That's my blood, not yours," Cam said, glancing at his arm. "I carved myself up on a broken bottle, thanks to you and your boss. Listen to me, hotdog. You tell Santini I want to see him. Now. Not a month from now, but pronto. Understand?"

"Yeah."

"You also inform him that the next one of his yo-yos I catch tailing me is going to end up in a body cast. Got that?"

"Yeah. Get off me, Porter. You're caving in my ribs."

"You're not in a position to be giving orders."

"So sit there and lose a bucket of blood. When you pass out, I'll dump your carcass in the ocean. That ought to make your lady's day."

"You tell Santini to stay away from Lisa!" Cam bellowed.

"Tell him yourself when you see him. Which you won't do unless you get off me so I can deliver your damn messages."

With a few well-chosen expletives, Cam got to his feet. He swore again, then pulled the ragged edges of his sweater tightly over the bleeding wound.

The man staggered to his feet and gingerly probed his neck before picking up the camera.

"I heard that you were good," the man said, "but it was a definite understatement. Sorry about your arm, Porter. Hell, I'm sorry about my own battered body. No one would believe we're on the same side. I'll deliver your message to Santini."

"Yeah," Cam said, his jaw tight, "you do that."

"Well, see you around. Forget it. I'll stay a lot healthier if I never see you again."

Cam watched until the man had disappeared into the darkness. Then he turned and started back down the beach, his hand still tightly clutching his bleeding arm.

One image, one thought, beat against Cam's mind: Lisa.

What was he going to say to her?

Where was Cam? Lisa's mind asked again and again.

When Cam had disappeared along the beach, Lisa's first thought had been to call the police to bring help for Cam in dealing with the man he was chasing. Lisa dismissed the frantic idea immediately. As quickly as everything had happened, and as frightened as she was, she somehow just knew that the police should not be brought into this.

Cam had known the man on the beach, Lisa realized, or at least known why he was there. What was going on?

And who and what was Cameron Porter?

Lisa paced back and forth at the bottom of the stairs, tears stinging her eyes. In the pit of her stomach there was a cold pain of fear that was accompanied by the cadence of the questions in her mind.

Yes, Cam had worked in dangerous areas of the world and knew how to protect himself. And he'd grown up streetwise and tough in a sleazy neighborhood in Los Angeles. But he was a civil-service employee and, no, damn it, they didn't go slinking around in the dark with infrared cameras taking pictures of one another. And, no, a man didn't react like a fine-tuned machine, streetwise or not, unless he'd been trained to face those who meant him harm.

Cam was involved in far more than bringing computer technology to hot spots around the globe. He was not who he had presented himself to be, Lisa knew, and the realization brought an ache to her heart and fresh tears to her eyes.

Emotions tumbled together and twisted within Lisa. She was sick with worry about what was happening to Cam at that moment, shattered by the force of his deception, and angry. Rip-roaring, totally ticked off, mad!

How dare Cameron be a phony!

How dare he be no better than that low-life Jim Weber.

How rotten Cam was for having kissed her, touched her, evoked passion in her like none she had ever known. And if he got himself killed out there on that beach, she'd punch him in the nose and never speak to him again.

The nerve of that man, that pirate, for making her fall in love with him.

"What?" Lisa whispered, standing statue-still. Oh, just wonderful. She was in love with Cameron Porter. What an asinine thing to do. She was going to wring his neck. And if he didn't show up safe and sound in the next two minutes, she was going to splinter into a million pieces.

Lisa's head snapped up as she saw a shadowy figure along the edge of the beach.

"Cam?" she said, her voice hushed. "Cam!" she yelled in the next instant, then started running toward him.

Cam's jaw tightened as he saw Lisa racing across the sand in his direction. He glanced at his arm, and knew he couldn't release the pressure of his hand. The cut was deep; blood was oozing between his fingers, had soaked the sleeve of his sweater and splattered onto his jeans. He looked terrible, and was probably going to scare Lisa to death.

And what was he going to say to her?

"Cam," Lisa said, gasping for breath as she skidded to a halt in front of him, "are you all right? What . . . Dear Lord, you're bleeding."

"I cut my arm on a broken bottle, that's all," he said, looking at his arm rather than at her.

"Come to the house so I can clean it up. Hurry. Come on."

Cam's frown deepened as he quickened his step. Lisa was in front of him, glancing over her shoulder as though checking to see that he was still there. He saw her pale features, her big green eyes, which seemed to radiate a mingled message of fear, confusion, and . . . what? That sudden flash he'd seen had been anger, then a flicker of pain. What was he doing to her? He had no right to hurt her this way.

Not Lisa, the only woman he had ever loved.

Cam stumbled slightly, then regained his footing, his mind whirling. He loved her? He sure did. Whatever doubts he may have had on the subject were gone.

He was in love with Lisa Peterson. There he was, looking like a refugee from a war zone, dripping blood on the silver sands of Malibu Beach, and realizing he was in love for the first time in his life. Sick. Really sick. So much for candlelight and roses. Cupid had a lousy sense of humor.

Lisa stopped at the bottom of the stairs and waited for him to reach her.

"Lisa," he said, "I'm a mess here. I can't go into your house like this. I'll just drive on back to Bret's and clean up. No sense in your getting involved."

That did it. "Involved?" Lisa said, her voice shrill. "Not get involved? Are you crazy? You fly off my deck like a close relation of Superman and come back looking like you've been run over by a truck. Your life's blood is dripping on my beach—mine!—but I shouldn't get involved?"

"Look, I—"

"Shut up, Porter!" she shrieked. "Don't tell me what you did to that man when you caught him, because I don't want to know. I don't want to know anything, except that you're not standing there dying because I've never seen so much blood in my life and..." Tears spilled onto Lisa's cheeks. "And I couldn't bear it if you died, but I hate you for not being what you said you were, and...and I love you with every breath in my body. Oh, get lost!"

Cam blinked slowly, opened his mouth, then snapped it closed. He shook his head slightly, then tried again.

"You love me?" he said, a smile creeping onto his face.

"No," she said, then sniffed.

"Yes, you do. You said it. I'll be damned," he said, the smile widening. "Well, guess what. I love you, too."

"Do people say weird things before they pass out from loss of blood?" Lisa said, squinting at him. "Should I call the paramedics?"

"I do love you, Lisa," Cam said, his voice low, his expression serious now. "I swear I do. And I'm more sorry than I can say about putting you through what happened here tonight."

"Oh, Cam," she said, nearly choking on a sob, "I don't know what to think, or do, or... or anything."

"Can you put it all on hold for now? I realize it's asking a lot, but I've got to get this arm tended to."

"Oh, your arm!" she said, quickly brushing the tears from her cheeks. "We've got to get you inside."

"No, I'm going to need a couple of stitches. Do you have an old towel I could wrap around it?"

"Yes, of course. Then I'll drive you to an emergency room."

"No."

"Yes. Just shut up again, okay? My nerves are really shot. I'll go get a towel and lock up the house. Meet me by the car."

"All right. Lisa, at the hospital, let me do the talking."

"I wouldn't dream of stealing your spotlight, Mr. Porter," she said, waving her hand in the air. "No one would believe me if I told them what happened, anyway. It sounds like a bad movie. Do you really love me?"

"Yes," he said, smiling warmly at her, "I do."

"Fancy that," she said, shaking her head. "I'll get the towel," she said in the next instant, then ran up the stairs.

"Put some shoes on," Cam called after her. "Oh, yes, I love you, Lisa," he said quietly, "and before this is over you may wish you'd never met me."

A deep frown knitting his dark brows together, Cam walked around the side of the house and leaned against his car. He gritted his teeth as a searing pain shot all the way up to his shoulder, and he silently called Santini several less-than-complimentary names.

What a mess, Cam thought, as a wave of utter fatigue swept through him. He was loved in return by the only woman he had ever loved, and he should be in a state of euphoria. Instead, he was up to his ears in trouble, and dragging people he cared about right into the middle of it. Bret would be ready to take him apart when he found out what Lisa had been subjected to. And Cam should just let Bret have at it.

"Let's go," Lisa said, coming out the front door. "Get in my car, then I'll wrap this towel around your arm."

"We'll use my car. Actually, it belongs to the Feds. Let them clean up the blood."

"I'm not going to argue the point," she said, coming to his side. "Move your hand... Oh, Cam, that looks awful."

"Pull the towel around it as tight as you can... Good. Open the door for me, will you? I need to keep pressure on this."

As Lisa drove away from the house, Cam sighed and leaned his head back.

"Are you all right?" she asked, glancing over at him quickly.

"I've been better. Then again, I've been worse."

"Don't tell me about the worse, not now," she said, shaking her head vigorously. "Later, maybe, but not now."

"Ah, Lisa, I really am so sorry. I owe you an explanation that I can't give you. That stinks, but there's nothing I can do about it at the moment. I'm going to work all this out, but I need some time. All I can tell you is that I love you."

"I love you, too," she said softly, "but..."

"But?" He lifted his head to look at her.

"I'm not sure I'm overly thrilled about it right now."

"Can't blame you for that, but everything is going to be fine. You'll see," he said. It had to be!

"I hope so," she said. It just had to be! "I'll tell you this. From now on, whatever gruesome junk happens to the pirates in my books, they're not going to bleed. Not a drop of blood will leave their bodies. I've seen enough tonight to last me a lifetime."

Cam smiled. "You're some kind of woman, Lisa Peterson," he said. "You really are. And I love you."

Lisa sighed, a deep, wobbly sigh, and they drove the remaining miles in silence.

At the hospital, Lisa stared up at Cam with wide eyes as he flashed the nurse on duty one of his hundred-watt smiles and delivered a smooth dissertation on how he had hurt his arm. They'd been playing with a Frisbee on the beach, Cam said, and son-of-a-gun if he hadn't tripped over his own big feet, klutz that he was, and taken a header, cutting his arm on a broken bottle. The nurse clucked sympathetically, batted her eyelashes, and went so far as to call Cam "you poor baby" before she whisked him off down the hall.

Cam grinned at a scowling Lisa over his shoulder, then gave her an ever-so-sexy wink. She stuck her tongue out at him. Then she sank into a leather chair in the waiting room and pressed her fingertips to her aching temples.

Maybe this was a nightmare and she'd wake up, she mused. No, that wasn't such a great idea. Then she would have only dreamed that Cam loved her. Cam loved her? Why should she believe his grand declaration, when he was cloaked in a cape of deception? How dramatic. But sadly true. So how did she know that he really loved her?

"Because I just know," she said aloud. Not bright. She'd believed Jim Weber when he'd said he loved her, and he'd been lying through his capped teeth. But Cam was...Cam. She'd never before experienced what she felt when he held and kissed her. But it was even more than the wondrous awakening of her femininity. Along with the churning desire within her was a quiet section of peace, contentment, of the greatest joy she had ever known. Yes, Cam loved her, and she loved him. It was glorious. And she was scared out of her wits.

Stop thinking, Lisa told herself. She was going to blank her mind for now and just sit there like a lump. She'd definitely had enough for one night. She should start being kinder to the pirates in her books, though. She just dragged them from one crisis to the next without the slightest regard for their mental well-being. A little rejuvenating sex here and there, of course, but still...

"Shut up, Lisa," she said. "You're babbling."

She leaned back in the chair and closed her eyes, willing herself not to think about anything heavier than whether she'd have a banana or an orange with her coffee the next morning. She was suddenly exhausted, and felt as though she weighed three hundred pounds. She was just drifting off into a dreamy state when warm, soft lips brushed over hers. Her eyes popped open and she found herself staring into the ebony depths of Cam's eyes, which were only an inch from hers.

"Come on, babe," he said, his voice floating over her like rich velvet. "Let's go home."

Five

It had taken a dozen stitches to close the gash on Cam's arm, plus that many in another row beneath the skin. The wound was covered in gauze, and he had been given a plastic wrap to use to keep it dry while he showered.

Cam insisted on driving, saying that Lisa looked exhausted and that it wouldn't hurt his arm as it was completely numb at the moment from the painkillers he'd been given. Lisa voiced no objection, and they started for home.

Lisa *was* all worn out, Cam thought, glancing over at her. She'd had a rough night, and it was his fault. What was she thinking regarding his refusal to give her an explanation for what had happened on the beach? What conclusions had she drawn? He was asking her to trust him on the basis of the fact that he'd told her that he loved her. Was it enough? Why should it be?

Lisa loved him, Cam mused. Incredible. He'd never considered the possibility that he'd love and be loved in return, just hadn't seen it in the cards for himself. And now here it was, in the form of Lisa. He wanted to kiss her, hold and touch her, make love to her through the night. They'd close the door on the world beyond the silver sands, and concentrate only on each other.

Fat chance, he continued silently, shaking his head slightly. He'd brought the world to Lisa's front door, in the form of Santini. Now what? How long would it take the joker with the camera to deliver Cam's messages to Santini and get the ball rolling? Cam wanted out now. He had no way of contacting Santini himself, had always waited to be approached by someone to receive new orders or report on the outcome of an assignment. Santini had called Cam on occasion, but was nothing more than a voice on the phone. Even back when Cam had originally been recruited, he hadn't personally met the man in charge of the agency.

Cam had told the man on the beach to let Santini know Cam wanted to see him. Would Santini bend his own rules to soothe his dissatisfied agent, to try to bring him back into the fold? And in the meantime, while that joker was going through channels to deliver Cam's messages, Cam was probably still being watched. And so were Lisa and Bret.

He should have done it differently, Cam realized. When he'd delivered his report after the last assignment, he'd voiced his intentions to sever his connection with Santini. He should have kept his mouth shut until his month's vacation was over, then announced his news flash. Well, what was done was done, and now he had to figure out what to do next.

There was a deep frown on Cam's face as he pulled up at Lisa's and turned off the ignition.

"Lisa," he said, turning to face her, "are you all right?"

"What? Oh, yes, I'm fine. I'm tired, that's all. You'd think that someone who writes adventure novels would be more prepared for this type of thing, but I guess it doesn't work that way."

"No, I'm sure it doesn't. Look, I'd really like you to stay at Bret's until I can get this mess straightened out."

"Why?" she said, frowning. "Whatever you're involved in has nothing to do with me."

"I'm afraid it does, because I've been spending time with you. I'm not saying you're in any danger, but I'm sure you're being watched. So is Bret. I never would've come here if I'd known it was going to be handled this way. But saying how sorry I am doesn't erase the fact that I've dragged you and Bret into a situation where you don't belong. I think you should go to Bret's."

"I'm not leaving my home, Cam. I don't know who it is that's watching me, but I haven't done anything wrong. I have a book to finish, and I'm staying right here."

"Bret has a computer you can use," he said. "Bret and I would both be there at night, then I'd stay close during the day."

"No," she said, opening the car door and sliding out.

Cam got out and met her at the front of the car. "Lisa, please, listen to me. I'm going to have all of this stopped—I promise you that—but in the meantime—"

"In the meantime, I have no clue as to what's going on," she interrupted him. "But I'm supposed to just pack up and leave because someone is watching me? No, thank you. I don't know who you are or what you've done. If I had any sense at all, I'd demand that you get out of here and never come near me again. But I love you, so my good sense is out the window. But I will *not* leave my home." She spun around and marched to the front door.

"She's tilting that stubborn Peterson chin in the air again," Cam muttered.

"You'd better believe it, Porter," she yelled over her shoulder.

Cam rolled his eyes heavenward and followed Lisa into the house.

But in the house there was only silence.

Lisa turned on every light in the living room, fluffed the throw pillows on the sofa, then straightened the magazines on the coffee table.

This was her home, her mind repeated, and she wasn't leaving. So what if the man she loved was being stalked by men with cameras, and probably guns, knives, and who knew what else. Big deal that those men were out there slinking around watching her, too. They didn't scare her. What a joke. She was petrified.

And her fear went deeper, all the way through her heart with a piercing pain, and on to her soul. On to the treasured place where she held fast to the knowledge that she loved Cam and he loved her.

Who was he, and what had he done?

Why were those men after him?

She had to be brave, mature, Lisa told herself. But she didn't want to be calm and reasonable, wait for the answers Cam had promised to give her when he could.

She wanted to rant and rave, demand that he explain now, then straighten out this horrifying mess thirty seconds after that. She wanted to be mad and sad and tell Cam he was a total pain in the kazoo. And she wanted him to hold her so tight, assure her that everything was fine, be who she had thought he was, then make love to her through the hours of the night.

"Lisa," Cam said gently.

"Would you like a drink?" she said, her voice quivering as she fought against sudden tears. She fluffed the pillows again, not looking at him. "Or a snack? I have some cheese, crackers, fresh fruit. We could make some popcorn, or—"

"Lisa," he said, moving slowly toward her.

"I think I'll have a bowl of cereal with bananas sliced on top. That sounds tasty, don't you think? Maybe some toast, too, with strawberry jelly."

Cam closed the distance between them and gripped her by the shoulders, turning her toward him. "Stop it," he said, giving her a small shake.

"Damn you," she sobbed, giving way to her tears. She pushed hard against his chest, but he tightened his hold. "Why couldn't you have been an ordinary, trustworthy pirate? Why weren't you real and honest? I hate you for making me love you. I don't want to love you. Do you understand? But how do I stop loving you?"

With a moan, Cam gathered her close, pressing one hand to her head and the other to her back. She buried her face in his sweater and wept. And he held her. He held her as though he'd never again let her go, each of her racking sobs like a knife twisting in his gut. He was filled with guilt and anger, frustration and pain.

And he was filled with love.

There in his arms was his Lisa, his life. Her tears were caused by him. She felt betrayed and frightened, and there was nothing he could do yet to change that. His love for her was bringing her nothing but grief, but he couldn't turn back the clock and pretend he hadn't brought his sordid world crashing down on her. It was too late to walk away from her. Santini knew about her; the damage was done.

Dear Lord, how he loved her. A shudder swept through Cam, and he buried his face in Lisa's fragrant hair. Her sobs were quieting as she gripped his sweater in her tight fists. She drew a long, uneven breath, then sniffled as he continued to hold her in the safe circle of his arms. She released her grasp on his sweater and slid her arms around his waist, moving even closer to his warmth and strength.

Cam lifted his head, Lisa lifted hers, and their eyes met. Cam sucked in his breath when he saw her tear-stained face.

"I'm so sorry," he said, his voice raspy with emotion. "I love you, Lisa. I never meant to hurt you. I've waited a lifetime for you without even realizing it, and I'm destroying everything we could've had together. I'll leave you alone, get out of your life, as soon as I can, but I've got to stay close to you until this is over."

"Get out of my life?" Lisa repeated, frowning up at him. "Leave me alone? Just sail away on your pirate ship?"

"I've caused you nothing but pain. I should never have come here, but I didn't know it would be handled this way. And I didn't know I'd fall in love with you and . . . I've made so many mistakes, it's sick."

"Loving me is a mistake?" she said, searching his face for an answer.

"For you, yes. Love isn't supposed to make you cry."

"That wasn't a ton of tears, only a few. Get out of my life? Leave? But I love you and you love me, and... You said you'd explain everything when you could and... Why are you talking about leaving me? For that matter, why are you talking at all? Please, Cam, just kiss me. Kiss me until I can't think. I want to feel you, taste you, know you're here with me, but I don't want to think."

With a strangled groan, Cam brought his mouth down hard on hers. A sob escaped her throat as she returned the kiss with feverish abandon. Cam's hands slid to her buttocks, pulling her up against him as his tongue delved deep into her mouth to be met by hers. A tremor swept through his body and the kiss intensified.

Cam tore his mouth from Lisa's and drew a ragged breath before kissing away the salty tears on her cheeks. Her eyes were closed as she savored the sensations of heated desire swirling within her. His hands moved up to roam over her back, molding her to him, crushing her breasts to the hard wall of his chest.

Lisa uttered a tiny, passion-laden sound; a purr, a moan, that ignited his desire nearly beyond his control. He sought her mouth again in a punishing kiss, and she answered in kind, their lips moving over each other's in urgent, frenzied motions. Their labored breathing echoed in the quiet room.

No! Cam's mind screamed. This was wrong. Lisa was frightened and vulnerable; she wasn't thinking clearly. He couldn't make love to her, not now, not like this.

"No," he gasped, lifting his head. "Lisa, no."

"I want you, Cam," she whispered. "I want you to make love to me."

With trembling hands he moved her gently away from him, then drew a deep, shuddering breath that seemed to tear at his soul. A muscle jumped along his jaw, and sweat trickled down his back.

"No," he said, his voice gritty. "Too much has happened tonight, Lisa. I don't want our lovemaking to be caught up in this nightmare. You're not thinking clearly, and I understand that. I've put you through hell. This isn't the right time for us. Don't you see?"

"No, I don't see," she said, her voice rising. "You're treating me like a child, instead of a woman who knows her own mind. You're calling all the shots here, and I resent that. You speak of loving me and leaving me in the same breath. What about *my* wants? *My* needs? Don't they count for anything? I want you to make love with me, Cameron, and I've never said that to a man in my entire life. But it's honest and real, and if it sounds pushy or brazen, that's just tough."

Cam frowned. "You were easier to deal with when you were crying," he said. "You've got some temper."

"Yes, I do, and I've used up my quota of sweetness for one day."

"You've also used up your quota of rational thinking," he said, raking his hand through his hair. "Go to bed, Lisa. I'll sleep out here on the sofa. I'll send a message to Bret over the modem asking him to come here in the morning so I can tell him . . . well, as much as I can tell him. Go on. You're exhausted."

"I'm not a child!" she yelled.

"That's enough," Cam said, his dark eyes flashing with anger. "I'm very aware of the fact that you're a woman, Lisa. I want you. I want to tear off your clothes and take you right here on the floor. I want to make love to you until we're too weak to move. I want to kiss and touch and taste every inch of you, and feel your hands on me, all of me."

"Oh," she said in a small voice.

"But this is not the night!" he roared. Lisa jumped. "I've got an ache in my gut that fifteen cold showers won't cure, but I'm still not going to touch you. You can throw a tantrum for the next hour straight, and I won't change my mind. I've got enough guilt eating at me, thank you. My arm is coming alive and hurts like hell, your brother is probably going to break my face, and I don't need this hassle! Now, get your backside in that bedroom before I pick you up and toss you in there!"

Lisa blinked several times before attempting to speak. "I do believe," she said finally, "that I will retire. It's been a rather taxing evening."

"That's a very wise decision on your part," Cam said, scowling at her.

"I'll get you a pillow and blanket."

"Fine. Goodbye."

"Would you like some aspirin for your arm?"

"If it wouldn't be too much trouble. I don't want to take those pain pills the doctor gave me. I'll go send a message to Bret," Cam said, starting across the room.

"Cam," Lisa said softly.

He stopped, his back to her. "Yeah?" he said.

"Thank you."

Cam stiffened and drew a deep breath. "Yeah," he grunted, then went down the hall.

"I love you," she whispered, then walked slowly out of the room.

Lisa made up the sofa with sheets, a blanket and pillow. She placed a fresh towel and a bottle of aspirin on the coffee table, then returned to her bedroom and closed the door.

Cam would not emerge from the computer room, she surmised, until he was assured she was tucked away for the night. He was at the limit of his self-control, and she knew it. What it must have taken for him to refuse what she had so brazenly offered him, she marveled. And he'd been right to send her away. She'd been behaving like the child she claimed she wasn't, actually pitching a fit and demanding he make love to her. How wrong it would have been to use their union as a means of escaping from the confusion and turmoil of the night.

Cam's rejection had spoken of his love for her, Lisa realized, of its depth and validity. He truly loved her, as she did him. She had to be patient, give him the time he needed to deal with the situation at hand. Whatever it was. She'd swallow her fears and wait. Wait for Cam.

Lisa showered, floated a soft nightie over her head, then slipped between the cool sheets with a weary sigh. Cam's image drifted before her eyes, and tingling fingers of desire traveled through her. He was just across the hall; so close, yet for now so far away. They were separated by the shadows of the unknown, the heavy weight of secrets and unanswered questions. Cam had recognized the importance of it all being put to rest before they reached out for each other. So be it. She would wait.

"He'll explain everything," Lisa said to the darkness, "then we'll get on with our lives. That's how it will go. It just has to. Oh, Cam, please."

Lisa pulled the blanket to her chin and stared up at nothing as a single tear slid down her cheek.

In the other bedroom, Cam tried calling Bret. Cam was not surprised there was no answer. Bret had more than hinted that his date that evening would end at dawn. Cam would have to use the modem and count on Bret coming home for clean clothes before he went to Peterson Computer, and seeing the printout of Cam's message.

BRET, Cam typed, SPENDING NIGHT ON LISA'S SOFA. BIT OF TROUBLE IN REGARD TO REFLEXES, ETC. THAT YOU PICKED UP ON. COME OVER HERE FOR BREAKFAST. FEEL FREE TO TAKE YOUR BEST SHOT. I'VE GOT IT COMING. CAM.

Cam punched in the necessary code, then pushed himself wearily to his feet, rotating his neck back and forth. His arm was really awake now, too, and throbbing like a hundred toothaches. Aspirin wasn't going to touch that pain, but he wasn't going to dope himself up with the pills the doc had given him. He was there to watch over Lisa, not pass out in a drugged sleep.

In the living room, Cam tugged off his shoes, then decided the idea of a shower was very appealing. He stopped outside Lisa's closed door for a long moment before he entered the bathroom at the end of the hall, taking Lisa with him in his mental vision.

A shower, four aspirins and a glass of milk later, Cam lay in the darkness on the sofa, clad only in his underwear.

Nobility was hell, he decided. Sexual frustration was *not* fun, cold showers were worthless, and he wanted to make love to Lisa Peterson. So much for that little inventory of tidbits. He should also, he thought, add the item that being in love was weird. What sane, red-blooded male would have backed away from the offer Lisa had made to him? Not many. But *he* had, old noble Porter, due to some newfound sense of right and wrong. Definitely weird.

What a night, Cam thought, running his hand over his face. He'd like three seconds alone with Santini, just long enough to break his jaw. No, Cam was the one who'd played it wrong, not Santini. About the only thing he'd done right lately was to be sleeping a room away from Lisa at that very moment. Too bad his body didn't approve of what his mind had decided on.

Lisa, he mused. He sure did love her. And he could lose her. He was a man with secrets, and at some time in her past she'd suffered at the hands of a man with secrets. The longer Cam had to keep silent the worse it would be. Santini had to get the lead out, free Cam from this tangled web. There was so much at stake: his love, his life, his Lisa. Their future together.

Future? What future? He hadn't taken his thoughts past the fact that he was in love for the first time in his life. Was he talking marriage here, babies, mortgage, station wagon? What a heavy trip. And he still had his career plans to settle and . . .

"Go to sleep, Porter, before you blow a fuse in your brain," Cam ordered himself.

The aspirins at last dulled the pain in Cam's arm enough that he was able to drift off into a restless slumber that was plagued by haunting dreams of ominous shadowy figures chasing him down a deserted beach.

The sound of his name penetrated the mist in Cam's mind and he groaned.

"Cam, wake up."

Cam opened his eyes and stared up at a frowning Bret.

"Hit me now while I'm horizontal," Cam said. "It'll save me the trouble of falling over."

"What is going on? That's blood on your clothes there on the floor. What's with your arm? Is Lisa all right?"

"Keep your voice down," Cam said, raising himself up to a sitting position. "She needs to sleep. It was a rough night." He reached for his jeans and tugged them on. "Oh, my aching body. Let's go in the kitchen and make some coffee. I'll fill you in, Bret, as best I can for now, which won't be much, I'm afraid."

"I got your computer message," Bret said, following him into the kitchen. "I'm not totally stupid, Cam. I'd already figured out that you'd been doing more than playing tiddlywinks with the Feds' computers. I'd put twenty on, shall we say, covert activities, secret-agent jazz?"

Cam spun around to face Bret, a deep frown accompanying his tightly clenched jaw.

"Relax," Bret said, pulling up a chair. "Make the coffee. How much does Lisa know?"

"Not much. Some yo-yo showed up on the beach last night with an infrared camera. The moon reflected off the lens, and I spotted him. I took off like a shot after him and carved up my arm on a broken bottle during our chat.''

"Why are they on your butt? Have you been a bad boy?''

"I want out, and they know it. Bret, I shouldn't be discussing this with you. I've already involved you and Lisa just by showing up here. I could really kick myself for that.''

"Don't worry about me. I have security clearance with the Feds that's probably as high as, if not higher than, yours. I've done some special programs for them. Lisa's not cleared, though. I got the contracts after she left Peterson Computer. So, okay, you're an agent, a spy who wants in from the cold. What happens next?''

"First they stall, watching me closely, of course, with the hope that I'll change my mind. If I don't, I'm debriefed, held somewhere until all the codes I know are changed and the agents I've dealt with are switched around. That's fine and dandy, except now Lisa's in the middle, and they may pull her in when I go.''

"Cute," Bret said, shaking his head. "You didn't give her any explanation for what happened last night?''

"No," Cam said, pouring two mugs of the steaming coffee. He set them on the table and sat down opposite Bret.

"Secrets," Bret said. "Not good. She has to be shook up. Well, maybe not. For all I know, she doesn't care about you.''

"Wrong.''

"Yeah, I figured as much. And you?''

"I love her, Bret. I really do," Cam said quietly.

Bret grinned. "I'll be damned," he said. "Love itself, huh? The biggie. When you go down for the count, you don't mess around. My sister and my best friend. Sounds good to me, buddy."

"Yeah, right," Cam said, scowling. "I'm a terrific guy for her. After all, look at the romantic evening we had last night."

"Don't be so hard on yourself. This will all straighten itself out."

"Bret, they're watching me, sticking like glue, and I figure they'll do the same to Lisa. You, apparently, are in the clear. I tried to get her to go to your place, but no soap. So I stayed here."

"On the sofa," Bret said, chuckling. "Cam Porter on the sofa. Unreal."

"Knock it off. Listen, I don't want Lisa hassled. I assured her that she was in no danger, but that she was being watched because of me. The worst that could happen is they'll pull her in when I go, then find out she doesn't know a thing and send her home."

"But in the meantime, you haven't told her what she needs to know about you, Cam."

"It's better this way. If I told her I was an agent, they'd find out she's aware of that. They might keep her during my entire debriefing, just to be on the safe side. I'm trying to protect her from some hotdog agent cornering her here, and from being hauled away and kept under wraps as long as I'll be."

"I get the picture," Bret said, nodding, "but I'm not sure you're doing this right. Lisa deals better in facts, honesty. She doesn't like games and secrets."

"It's risky. I realize that. She might end up hating my guts. But I still feel it's the best way to do it. Do I have your word you won't tell her?"

"Yeah. I know you'll take good care of her. I only hope you've made the right decision. I wouldn't make book on it, though."

"We'll see. I've got the word out that I want to talk to the boss pronto. The sooner this is over, the better."

"That's no joke. You'll be staying here, then?"

"If Lisa doesn't toss me out on my butt," Cam said, smiling slightly. "She's got some temper when she gets going."

"Your being here will guarantee she'll get hauled in for questioning."

"But she won't know anything," Cam said, leaning toward him. "That's what I'm counting on. Those guys are sharp. They'll know she's telling the truth. I just don't want one popping out of her closet and scaring her to death. They won't be able to get near her unless it's all done officially. They'll quiz her, bring her back home. End of story."

"Yeah, but what about the Lisa-and-Cam story? How is that going to end?"

"I wish I knew, Bret."

"Cam?" Lisa called, then appeared in the kitchen a moment later, dressed in jeans and a green knit top. "Oh, Bret, you're here, too."

"Hi, kid," Bret said, getting up and kissing her on the cheek. "Sit. I'll pour you a cup of coffee."

"Thank you," she said absently. She sank onto a chair, acutely aware of her trembling knees. Dear heaven above, she thought wildly, Cam Porter without a shirt. It was too much, it really was. Such beautifully proportioned muscles, and that dark curly chest hair, the taut, tanned skin and . . . really too much.

"Good morning," Cam said quietly.

Lisa met his gaze, feeling the warm blush on her cheeks as she realized she'd been staring at his bare chest.

"Good morning, Cam," she said. Hello, my love, her mind whispered. Oh, yes, she did love this man. Be it right or wrong, she loved him. "How's your arm?"

"Fine."

"I doubt that," she said, shifting her gaze from his compelling dark eyes. "I...your shoulder. Is that scar from where you were shot?"

Cam glanced at his shoulder. "Old news, remember?" he said, smiling at her.

"Coffee," Bret said, placing a mug in front of Lisa. He sat down at the end of the table. "Well, children, how's life?" he said, grinning at them.

"Fascinating," Lisa said dryly. "Just one laugh after the next."

"So I hear," Bret said. "How about moving to my place for a while, sister mine?"

"No."

"I tried," Bret said to Cam with a shrug.

"Lisa," Cam said, "it really would be best if you went to Bret's."

"No."

"Hell," Cam said, slouching back in his chair. Bret chuckled.

"You're awfully calm about all this, Bret," Lisa said, frowning. "Why do I get the feeling you know more than I do?"

"I've always known more than you do," he said, wiggling his eyebrows at her. "I've been telling you that since you were six years old, dumdum."

"You know what I mean," she said, her voice rising. "You two have had a big macho meeting out here, haven't you? You've decided to protect little Lisa from the nasty facts of life.''

"Calm down, okay?" Cam said, reaching for her hand.

"No, I will not calm down," she said, whacking him on the knuckles with a spoon. "Don't patronize me. I'm a grown woman, Cameron."

"Don't start that again," he groaned. "We covered that ground."

"Last chance," Bret said. "Will you move to my place, brat?"

"No!"

"Okay, Cam," Bret said, "I'll wait here while you go get your stuff, then I've got to hustle to the office."

"Stuff? What stuff?" Lisa said.

"I won't be long," Cam said, draining his mug, then getting to his feet. "I'll shower, shave, pack a few things."

"Leaving town, are you?" Lisa said sweetly. "How nice."

"I'm moving in here, Miss Sunshine," Cam said, glaring at her.

"You certainly are not," she said, jumping to her feet.

Cam slid his hand to the nape of her neck, then kissed her hard on the mouth.

"I certainly am," he said, close to her lips. "Be back in a flash," he added as he strode out of the room.

"Bret," Lisa said, spinning around to face her brother, "do something. I can't believe that you're just going to sit there and allow—"

"Sit down, sweetheart," he said gently. "Come on."

Lisa threw up her hands and sank back down on her chair.

"I love him, Bret," she said with a sigh. "I'm in love with Cam."

"Yeah, I know."

"It's like déjà vu."

"No, Lisa, it's not. Cam isn't Jim Weber. I realize there are things about Cam that you don't know, but it has to be this way."

"Why? He says that he loves me. Love is supposed to be based on honesty, trust, all the rest of it. Cam is keeping things from me, and I hate that. It's like being in a bad movie and not even knowing my role. Love can be crushed by the weight of secrets."

"If you love Cam, then trust him. That's all I can say to you, Lisa."

"You know what he's keeping from me, don't you?"

"Yeah."

"Damn it, Bret, I'm your sister."

"Do you think this is easy for me? I've been hovering over you since you could walk. But Lisa, it's time I stepped back and faced the fact that you're all grown up. Okay, the last time I did it, Weber fooled us both. But this is Cam. He's my best friend, one of the finest men I know. He loves you; you love him. I've got to respect you both enough to stay out of this. I'm trusting him with you. Why can't you do the same thing? Give the guy some time to get this mess straightened out."

Lisa got slowly to her feet, then picked up her coffee mug and cradled it in her hands.

"I'm terribly frightened, Bret," she said, her voice hushed. "And I hate secrets. I really hate secrets."

"Ah, Lisa," Bret said, shaking his head.

"I've got to get to work," she said, then turned and walked from the room.

Lisa sat down in front of the computer and went through the motions of loading a disk. The screen was soon filled with the text of her book, and she pressed the key to move the pages, bringing her up to the point where she was supposed to add the next line.

"Ha," she muttered. She was in no position to solve the problems between the pirate and his maiden, not when her own life was a jumbled maze. "Where's your professionalism, Jasmine?" she said aloud. "Write your little heart out."

To her own amazement, Lisa became completely engrossed in the story, her fingers flying over the keys. A short time later, she heard the low rumble of male voices and surmised that Cam was back with his ever-famous stuff. Forcing herself to concentrate, she typed on, losing herself in another era. She became the pirate and the maiden, blocking all thoughts of herself and Cam from her mind.

"Lisa," Cam said from the doorway.

"You scared me," she said, jumping in her chair.

"I'm sorry. I guess I'm not supposed to interrupt you when the creative juices are flowing or whatever, but you haven't had anything to eat."

She swiveled to face him, and her pulse skittered at the sight of his magnificent body clad in tan cords and a dark brown knit shirt.

"I don't always eat breakfast," she said, deciding to examine the toe of her tennis shoe.

"I'm talking about lunch. It's two o'clock."

"You're kidding," she said, looking at him again.

"I fixed you something. Come and eat, all right?"

"My, my," she said, her voice dripping with sarcasm as she got to her feet, "is that part of your babysitting service, Cam? I get my meals prepared? What else do you do?" she said, walking to where he stood. "Tuck me in bed at night and read me a story? Providing, of course, that I've been a good little girl."

"Damn you," he said harshly, gripping her by the upper arms.

And in the next instant, his mouth swept down over hers.

Six

The force of the kiss spoke of Cam's frustration and anger, of a man pushed to the limits of his physical and emotional control. It was rough and bruising, then suddenly gentle.

Lisa felt the change and relaxed in Cam's arms, responding to his kiss and calling herself a fool for taunting him. She savored the taste and feel and aroma of him. Nothing mattered but the moment, the heat of it, the want and need, there in the safe haven of Cam's embrace. Her body was humming with desire, with a sweet ache that could be soothed only by the masculine promise of Cam. How she wanted him. And loved him.

"Ah, Lisa," Cam said, his voice gritty, "I want you so much. I kiss you, and I can't stop. I should go for a run on the beach, but I don't want to leave you here alone."

"You certainly talk a lot," she said, undoing the three buttons of his knit shirt.

"Don't," he said, grasping her hand. "Go eat your lunch."

"You're bossy, too," she said, pulling his shirt free of his pants. She slid her hands beneath the cloth and upward through the curly mass of moist hair on his chest, feeling him shudder at her feathery touch. "So strong," she whispered.

"Lisa, please, don't," Cam said, his voice sounding strangled. "I can't take this right now."

Lisa stilled her hands and gazed up at him, seeing the tight set to his jaw, the sheen of sweat on his brow, the smoky hue of desire reflected in the dark pools of his eyes. The love in her heart was matched by resolve.

"I love you, Cam," she said. "I'm frightened and angered by what's taking place around us, but that doesn't change the fact that I love you. I don't know what tomorrow is going to bring, because you won't tell me anything. So I'm living for now, this moment. And I want you."

"Lisa, I . . ."

"Can't I have that much, Cam? A moment? Is what's happening beyond that door so important that you can't put it away even long enough to make love with me?" she said, her hands resuming their tantalizing journey.

Think, Porter, Cam's mind raged at him. Did he have the right to touch her, now, in the midst of this nightmare? No. Yes. He didn't know. Did she realize what she was doing? Damn right she did. She was seducing the hell out of him with her stubborn little chin poked up in the air. How he loved her, wanted her, ached with the need of this woman.

"Love me, Cam," Lisa said. "You do want me, don't you?" Her fingertips inched below the waistband at the front of his cords.

"Sweet heaven," he rasped, sinking his hands into her hair, "you're killing me! Yes, I want you. And, yes, I'm going to make love to you right now. But not for a moment, for hours. Got that?"

"Oh, thank goodness," she said, smiling at him. "I've never tried to seduce a man before, and I had no idea how I was doing."

"Believe me, you did more than fine. But, Lisa, are you really sure you—"

"Darn it, do I have to start all over? A woman's work is never done."

Cam chuckled, then lifted her into his arms. "I surrender," he said. "I'll probably lose my pirate's license, but I'm putty in your hands, fair maiden."

"I love you, Cameron," she said softly, lacing her fingers behind his neck.

"And I love you," he said, his expression serious again. "Nothing matters right now but the two of us and what we're about to share."

Tears misted Lisa's eyes as she smiled at Cam. He carried her into the bedroom and set her on her feet. Then, cradling her face in his large hands, he kissed her so softly, so gently and sensuously, that a sob caught in her throat.

Yes, Lisa's heart and mind echoed, it was time. Time to trust, and time to be one with this man, her Cameron. Whatever they had to face later, out there beyond the silver sands, they would do it together. But now it was just the two of them and the moment.

With slightly trembling hands, Cam drew her shirt up and away, then removed her bra. His sharp intake of breath was audible in the quiet room as he filled his vision with the sight of her lush breasts. He cupped them in his hands, thumbs stroking the nipples to taut buds. Then he lowered his head to take first one, then the other, into his mouth. The blood pounded through his veins like hot lava. The sound of his thundering heart roared in his ears.

With reluctance and forced restraint, Cam lifted his head from the sweet flesh and placed Lisa on the bed. He pulled off her shoes, then slowly drew her jeans and panties down her slender legs.

"Ah, Lisa," he said, his voice hoarse, "you're beautiful, so beautiful."

Cam stood and shed his clothing, the stark white of the gauze on his arm contrasting sharply with the rich tan of his body. A body that was muscled and tight, powerful, and the most magnificent sight Lisa had ever seen. Her gaze swept over him from head to toe, as if she were etching him indelibly in her mind.

Her pirate, Lisa mused dreamily. Hers. Such promise his body held, such masculine strength, a strength she knew he would temper with gentleness.

"Cam," she whispered, lifting her arms to him.

He stretched out next to her and kissed her deeply before his mouth sought her breasts once again. As his lips, tongue, and teeth paid homage to the bounty offered him, his hands roamed over her lissome form.

Lisa, too, touched, explored, discovered the mysteries of Cam's body, her hands igniting a heated path as they traveled over steely muscles and moist skin. She felt him tremble with passion and restraint as he continued his foray.

Cam claimed her mouth again, his tongue delving within, meeting hers. She moaned softly and he caught the whisper of sound in his own mouth, matching it with a groan from deep within his chest. With every ounce of self-control he possessed, he held back, wanting, needing, to be sure that Lisa was ready to receive all he would give to her. His hand slid down her body, and she arched against him, telling him what he desperately needed to know.

"Cam, please," she gasped.

He moved above her, resting on his arms as he gazed at her flushed face. The smoky hue of her emerald eyes radiated her message of desire, and he smiled his satisfaction at the knowledge that she wanted him as much as he did her.

"I love you," he said, his voice unsteady.

"Come to me, Cam."

Slowly, tentatively, he entered her, watching her face, giving her body time to accept him. He had never before been so aware of his own strength compared to the fragile woman beneath him. Desire ripped through him as he held himself in check.

Lisa felt his restraint, saw the tight set to his jaw, the beads of sweat on his face. He was putting her first, she knew, and her heart nearly burst with love for him. But she needed and wanted him, all of him. Now.

Lisa lifted her hips as she gripped Cam's shoulders. He groaned, his control shattered by the sensuous movement. He thrust deep within her, and she sighed her pleasure, closing her eyes to savor the sensations rocketing through her.

"Oh, yes," she whispered.

They moved as one in a pounding rhythm that increased in tempo as passions soared. Gentleness was forgotten as the cadence grew stronger and harder, carrying them up and away. Seeking. Struggling. Reaching. Finding.

They toppled over the edge of oblivion only seconds apart, waves of release sweeping through them with the power of a raging tide.

Then peace.

A lingering there in the treasured place, then a slow descent in a hazy mist of sated contentment.

Cam buried his face in Lisa's fragrant curls, then pushed himself up to rest on his arms. She lifted her eyes to meet his gaze, and no words were spoken. They simply looked at each other, sending and receiving missives of wonder at what they had shared. And messages of love so clear it was as though they were shouting them to the heavens. Hearts quieted, bodies cooled, but they stayed as one.

"I don't know what to say to you," Cam said finally.

"I know. I feel the same way. I never dreamed it could be so... There aren't words, Cam."

"I should get off you, but you feel so good, *so good*."

"Don't go," she said, lacing her hands behind his neck. "Unless it hurts your arm to lean on it like that."

"What arm?" he said, nuzzling her neck. "You taste sweet, like nectar."

Lisa lifted her head to flick her tongue along his shoulder. "You taste salty, like a pretzel," she said.

"Oh, okay" he said, chuckling. The sound rumbled up from deep in his chest, and Lisa shivered from the sensation. "All you need to go with me is a beer," he said.

"All I need is you, Cam. Period. I love you so much."

"And I love you. I really am going to get off you now, before I smash you flat."

"Well, you should kiss me goodbye."

"If I do, I won't leave."

"That's the idea, Porter."

"No kidding, Peterson? Are you seducing me again?"

"You'd better believe it."

"I like the way your mind works."

"Only my mind?"

"Among other things," he said, lowering his lips to hers. "The list is endless."

Much, much later, they showered and dressed, then Cam grabbed Lisa by the hand and marched her into the kitchen. She was going to eat, he stated firmly, before she passed out from hunger. He served her a huge plateful of the fruit salad he'd prepared, along with flaky biscuits. Lisa told him he was a handy guy to have around. The look he gave her then was so blatantly sexual that she blushed crimson and punched him on the shoulder. Cam poured himself a cup of coffee and sat opposite her at the table while she ate.

"This book you're working on," he said, "does it have a due date, or deadline, or whatever they call it?"

"Yes. There's always a deadline. It's written into my contract."

"Where do you stand?"

"Ahead of schedule. If I put in another solid day of work, I'll have it wrapped up. Then I'll go through the whole book once more to make minor changes here and there, print it out, and mail it to my agent."

"So maybe two days max if you pressed?"

"Well, yes, I guess so. Why?"

Cam frowned. "Because I don't know what's going to happen or when, and I'd hate to mess up your writing career on top of everything else."

"Oh," Lisa said softly, "I see. Back to reality."

"Hey, don't look so sad," he said, smiling at her. "Everything is going to be fine."

"But you won't tell me what it's all about."

"It's better this way, Lisa," he said, frowning again. "It really is."

"All right, Cam," she said, sighing. Secrets. Even now, after what they had shared, he was keeping his secrets. Why couldn't Cam understand how wrong that was? Didn't he believe in her love enough to realize she would stand by him no matter what he told her about himself? But she had secrets, too. She had never confided in him about... "Jim Weber," she said.

"What?"

"His name was Jim Weber. Well, it wasn't really, but that was the name he used."

"The man, the one who hurt you," Cam said, his jaw tightening.

"Yes. You see, Cam, I had concentrated on my studies at MIT. For all my smarts, I was terribly naive, unworldly. I had just never had time for much of a social life. When I needed to unwind, I wrote my stories. Bret was concerned because I led such a narrow existence, and when Jim Weber showed up at Peterson Computer after I had gone to work there, Bret encouraged Jim's interest in me."

"Weber came to Peterson Computer?"

"He had phony references as a programmer. It was a sophisticated plan, because when Bret checked him

out, everyone he contacted raved about Jim. It was
very clever. They rented a room, had a bunch of phone
lines brought in, and Bret thought he was calling a
whole slew of different companies."

"Go on," Cam said, nodding.

"Jim really was a talented programmer. He worked
hard, was charming, good-looking, and swept me off
my naive feet. He loved me, he said, wanted to marry
me, and..." Lisa stopped talking and drew an uneven breath. "And it was all lies."

"Damn," Cam grated. "Why?"

"Industrial espionage. Bret and I were working on
a program together that was going to be a break-
through in toxic-waste readings in water systems. It
would mean being able to detect potentially dangerous areas before they were out of control. Bret and I
were the only ones involved, but while we kept it under wraps, we did mention the general concept to the
others at Peterson Computer."

"And someone sold you out."

"Yes. Jim bribed one of our people. Then wonderful Mr. Weber moved in for the kill. He wined and
dined me and bided his time. He'd ask casual questions about how the program was coming along, but
he didn't overdo his show of interest. One night I was
very excited because Bret and I had finished it at last.
Jim took me out to celebrate."

"And?"

"He begged me to let him see the program, said he'd
never had a glimpse of anything that complex and
technical. Like a fool, I took him to Peterson Computer and got the disks out of the safe. He—he
grabbed them from my hands, then laughed. It was the
most chilling laugh I had ever heard."

Cam's hands curled into tight fists on the top of the table as he saw the pain cross Lisa's face and settle in her eyes. He clenched his teeth until they ached, but he kept silent as he tried to control his raging anger.

"I was devastated. I can't begin to tell you what his betrayal did to me. I couldn't work, sleep, eat. I finally lost myself in writing and told Bret I was taking some time off from Peterson Computer."

"And Weber?" Cam asked.

"Bret and I had a safety code at the beginning of the program. It appeared to be very ordinary, but actually it wasn't. Well, you understand computers. We layered codes one over the other. Unless you went into the program in the proper order, it activated the command to erase the disk. Jim erased the disks, the idiot."

"And Bret had another copy."

"Of course. The people Jim worked for were furious at him, and he panicked. He threatened his contact at Peterson Computer, demanding that the man break into Bret's safe. That ticked off the creep, and he came to Bret. Bret set up a plan with the police, and eventually everyone connected with the deal was caught. Jim Weber and friends are in jail."

"But you never went back to Peterson Computer."

"No, Cam, I didn't. What had been therapy for me in the form of my writing became a tremendous new challenge. I slowly recovered from Jim's betrayal and began to grow as a person, as a woman. I traveled to New York to meet with my agent and editor, found a social life, friends, here in Malibu, that have enriched my life. My books bring pleasure to people. My characters are real to me. It's much more rewarding than dealing in equations."

"But those characters *aren't* real, Lisa. They're make-believe, a part of a fantasy. You're capable of creating programs that would benefit the multitudes, as proven by the toxic-waste project. How can you justify... No, I'm sorry. I have no right to stand in judgment of your career choice."

"No, you don't," she said coolly. "No one does."

"Lisa, why did you choose today to tell me about Weber?"

"Because it was my secret, and I didn't want it standing between us," she said, looking at him steadily.

"Cheap shot," he said, dragging his hand through his hair. "Look, I'm sorry you suffered through what you did, I really am. But I'm not Jim Weber, Lisa. I have never lied to you. Yes, I'm withholding facts from you, but I sincerely believe this is the best way. I have no intention of changing my mind on the subject."

A dull pain thudded in Lisa's chest, and tears stung at the backs of her eyes. She averted her gaze from Cam's and pushed the last pieces of fruit around on her plate with her fork.

So much for that, she thought dismally. Cam wouldn't give an inch. He was protecting her from the truth about himself, and that was wrong. Still, she was glad she'd told him about Jim Weber. It was out in the open now, over, finished.

But when would Cam be free? When did this cloud hanging over them get blown into oblivion? And why wouldn't he tell her his secrets?

"I'll clean up here if you want to get back to work," Cam said quietly.

"Yes, thank you, I will," she said, getting to her feet. "The lunch was delicious. Or was that dinner?"

"Dinner, I guess. We're on a rather strange schedule. Lisa?"

"Yes?"

"Today has been wonderful. Please don't let any of this other stuff take away from what we shared. It was beautiful, it was special, and it was ours."

Lisa managed a small smile, then turned and walked from the room.

Cam muttered an oath. He was hurting her with his silence, and it was ripping him apart. But he had to do it this way! If Santini didn't contact him soon, Cam was going to go straight out of his mind. He had to get this mess over with before it destroyed everything he had with Lisa.

Their lovemaking had been absolutely incredible, like nothing he had ever experienced before. They had held no portion of themselves back, had given, then received, totally of each other. Such a sense of completeness he had felt with Lisa, as though he were at last a whole man, sound of body, mind and soul.

Lord, how he loved her. And he was hurting her. And he couldn't do a thing about it. If he got the chance, maybe he'd bust Santini's jaw after all. Actually, the guy he'd really like to take apart was that low-life Weber. That jerk should count himself lucky that the police got him before Bret did. Bret must have been ready to kill him for what he did to Lisa.

"What he did to Lisa," Cam repeated aloud. The pain he had seen in her eyes as she left the kitchen had been caused by him, Cam Porter. Lisa had probably figured out he was trying to protect her, which would spark her fiery temper and bring on her "I am a woman" spiel. Yes, he was protecting her, and no, he wasn't going to tell her about himself. And, yes, he was hurting her, and he hated every minute of it. "Santini," Cam growled, "get off your butt."

Muttering expletives in three foreign languages, Cam began to clean up the kitchen.

Cam watched the vibrant colors of the sunset streak the sky. He stood on the deck, filling his lungs with the salty sea air, then scanned the beach for any sign of intruders. He saw no one.

But they were out there, he knew. Watching. So, okay, they had a job to do, but he had a life to lead, and enough was enough. There had to be some way to speed things up.

"Cam?" Lisa called from inside. "Are you on the deck?"

"Yeah. Come look at this sunset."

"Breathtaking," she said, joining him at the railing. "Hello."

"Hi," he said, smiling down at her. "You really worked hard today. Would you like to go out for something to eat?"

"Out?"

"You're not a prisoner here. I just don't want you to be alone. How does junk food sound? Greasy hamburgers and thick milk shakes."

"You're on."

"Your shoes aren't."

"I know exactly where I left them. Be back in a jiffy."

"Hold it," he said, pulling her into his arms. "You forgot something."

The kiss was long and sensuous, and Lisa's breathing was erratic when she finally dashed back into the house for her shoes. Cam scanned the beach once more, rapped his knuckles on the railing in a gesture of frustration, then went inside.

Cam chose the location of the fast-food restaurant with a definite purpose and a surge of guilt. The establishment was busy, crowded and had three separate entrances. Cam parked a block away, telling Lisa it was a nice night for a stroll. Even if there were two agents watching him, he reasoned, one would have to stay with the car. The other would be forced to go inside the restaurant. The risk of Cam's leaving through another door and simply never returning to his car was too great. He was pushing their buttons, doing it his way, but he felt guilty for moving Lisa around like a pawn.

Lisa slid into a booth while Cam waited in line to place their orders. Hunkering down to tie his shoe gave him a chance to glance around, as did stopping at a side counter for extra napkins. He purposely forgot the straws for the milk shakes and made a wide circle to retrieve them.

And then Cam saw him.

It took an agent to spot an agent, Santini had said once. And how true it was. Cam nearly laughed aloud at the ease with which he'd pegged the man in the crowd. Eyes that never quite stopped flickering around; a windbreaker that was too warm for the place, zipped one-third of the way up for easy access to the gun in the shoulder holster; a slight rocking forward on the balls of the feet—the guy was for real. No doubt about it.

Cam slid into the booth opposite Lisa and handed her a straw.

"I guess I finally got everything," he said. "How's your hamburger?"

"It's so awful, it's wonderful," she said, smiling. "Everyone should eat this ick occasionally so their stomach doesn't get complacent."

"Yep," he said, taking a bite of his. He hoped the agent got indigestion.

"There's someone here, isn't there?" Lisa said quietly.

"There're a lot of someones here. This place does a booming business."

"You know what I mean. We're being watched, right? We were followed from my house, and whoever it is, is in here."

"Oh, well, I don't..." Cam started. He couldn't lie to her. Something had to make him better than Weber. "Yeah," he said, nodding, "he's here. Keep eating. Smile if you think you can manage it. Try to act natural."

"Where is he?" Lisa whispered, leaning toward him.

"That's natural?" Cam said, laughing. "You're really great at this, kid."

"Oh, sorry," she said, moving back and smiling brightly. "How's this?"

"Phony. Take a bite of your hamburger."

"Well, for Pete's sake," she said, then took a bite.

"Up front, okay? I picked this place on purpose to bring him out in the open. They're moving too slow for my present state of mind."

"Check," Lisa said, narrowing her eyes. "What's the plan, Sam?"

"Oh, good Lord," Cam said, whooping with laughter. "You're too much."

Lisa frowned. "I thought this was all serious business," she said.

"It is," he said, still chuckling. "I'm getting my act together right now. I hope. Maybe I'll just pass on this guy."

"Cam, no. If there's any way to get this thing over with, then do it."

"I feel guilty enough about setting you up like this. It isn't fair."

"Says you, not me. Shh, he's coming this way."

"I beg your pardon?" Cam said, his eyes widening.

"Hush," she said. "And," she went on, "I said to my editor, 'Darling, you just don't understand the temperament of us creative people. Writers are sensitive, fragile, and—' Where did he go?"

"To a table in the corner. Lisa, how did you know who he was?"

"That jacket of his is too hot for this weather. He's carrying a gun, which doesn't do a lot for my nervous system. Also, he stopped at the side counter but didn't take one thing for his tray. He just looked around the place. Cam, close your mouth."

He loved this woman with every breath in his body, Cam thought, snapping his mouth shut. She was really something. How he wanted to pour the whole story out to her, erase her doubts, her fears, her hurt. She was being so brave sitting there acting like a supersleuth. She deserved better than what he was doing to her. But he couldn't let her go. He just couldn't.

"Cam?" Lisa said, jiggling his arm.

"What? Hey, that was very sharp of you to tag our friend. Unbelievable, in fact."

"Are you going to talk to him in here?"

"No."

"Why not? He's not going to pull his gun on you, is he?"

"No."

"That's comforting. Is there a rule about that?"

"No, I simply don't intend to allow him to have the opportunity to reach for his gun."

"Oh," Lisa said, and gulped.

"I'll tell you what. How would you like a speaking part to play when I nab our buddy?"

"Like 'Up against the wall, you slime'? Sure, I can handle that."

"No, Lisa," Cam said, shaking his head. "More on the order of 'What's going on here?' or 'What is the meaning of this outrage?'"

"That's really corny, Cam."

He frowned. "Well, you're the writer," he said. "Come up with something that indicates you have no idea what's happening. We're emphasizing your ignorance."

"Oh, thanks."

"We really are. It's important that you don't know a thing. It's not our fault this dingdong sticks out like a sore thumb. You just have to pretend you don't realize what he is."

"I don't know what he is, except that he's one of whoever they are."

"Look, let's forget this screwball plan. I don't want you—"

"So help me, Cameron," Lisa interrupted him, "if you say 'involved,' you're going to get the rest of this milk shake in your lap."

Cam sighed. "Yeah, I know I've involved you in this, and I'm mad at myself about it. Okay, we'll go for it," he said. "It wouldn't hurt the cause any to have you sound very confused and upset outside."

"Check."

"Are we back to that?" he said, smiling at her. "Well, are you ready?"

"Now?" she said, wondering absently if her voice was as squeaky as it sounded to her.

"Might as well get it over with. I really don't think this is a red-hot idea."

"Too bad," she said, sliding out of the booth. "All systems are go."

"Mmm," he said, frowning at her.

Cam took the tray full of debris to the trash container, returned the tray to the designated place, then wove his way back across the room to Lisa. He placed his fingertips lightly on her elbow and nodded toward the side entrance, which was directly opposite the agent's table.

When they were outside, Cam made a production of pointing to the Big Dipper and asking Lisa if she could see it clearly. They moved slowly along the sidewalk to the rear of the building. Cam pulled Lisa around the edge, flattened her against the wall and pressed his lips to hers. She stared at him in wide-eyed shock.

"Kiss me, you sexy number you," he said, trying to suppress a smile.

Lisa crossed her eyes and puckered up. Laughter rumbled up from Cam's chest, then he suddenly stiffened.

"Here we go," he said in a low voice.

Lisa gasped as Cam shifted his weight, reached around the side of the building, and hauled in an obviously surprised man. Lisa scooted out of the way as Cam shoved the man against the wall and gripped him by the throat.

"A mugger! A mugger! A mugger!" Lisa yelled, hands flying to her cheeks.

"Tell him I said 'now,' " Cam said to the man.

"Oh! Oh! I am so very frightened," Lisa said.

"Understand?" Cam said, tightening his grip.

"Yeah, yeah, I'll tell him," the man said, glaring at him. "Lighten up."

"He's out of time. Make that clear," Cam said, then backed away.

"Mercy, I'm going to faint," Lisa said, slapping the back of her hand to her forehead and rolling her eyes.

"You've got yourself a real nut case there, Porter," the man said, eyeing Lisa warily.

"Hit the road," Cam said through gritted teeth. The man disappeared into the darkness.

"A nut case," Lisa said, planting her hands on her hips. "The nerve of that man. I thought I did a perfectly reasonable impersonation of a damsel in distress."

Cam smiled and drew her into the circle of his arms. "You were Academy Award material," he said. "Now will you kiss me?"

"Am I still a sexy number?"

"Absolutely."

"Kiss away, Porter."

"My pleasure, Peterson."

The kiss seemed to steal the breath from Lisa's body, and she forgot where she was as she returned the kiss with total abandon, molding herself to Cam's rugged length.

"Lisa," he gasped, jerking his head up.

"Hmm?"

"We're in an alley by a trash dumpster. Why don't we head for our silver sands?"

"What? Oh, good grief."

"Come on," he said, pulling her close to his side.

They walked to the car in silence, lost in thought.

"Cam," Lisa finally said as he drove through the heavy traffic, "what happens now?"

"I wait."

"That's all you can do?"

"That, and hope that bozo reports that Lisa Peterson is such a nut case that she couldn't possibly know that I'm . . . couldn't know anything."

"Want to hear what I think?"

"Sure," he said, glancing over at her.

"I think you're a secret agent for the United States Government."

Seven

Damn," Cam roared, smacking the steering wheel with the palm of his hand.

"Bingo," Lisa said merrily. "I got it."

"Not another word," Cam said, jaw clenched. "Don't say one more word until we get to the house."

"Okay," Lisa said, shrugging. "We good guys always follow orders."

"Lisa!"

"Okay!"

The remaining distance to the house was covered in total silence.

In the living room, Cam pointed at the sofa and Lisa sat down, folding her hands primly in her lap.

"How?" he said, a deep scowl on his face. "How did you figure it out?" He stood in front of her, his hands on his narrow hips.

"I simply gathered my data, then assembled it, much as one would for a spreadsheet, and computed. The only piece missing is why they're so bugged at one of their own guys. I have two theories on that. Want to hear them?"

"I wouldn't miss it for the world," Cam said dryly.

"Well, theory number one," Lisa said pleasantly, "is that you screwed up an assignment."

"I certainly did not!"

"Check. On to theory number two. Since you are obviously so eager to speak to someone I assume is your superior, you must have an important message to deliver. Since you've voiced some dissatisfaction with your career and are considering joining Peterson Computer, I surmise you intend to terminate your relationship with them and they're none too pleased. How's that?"

Cam muttered an expletive, raking his hand through his hair. "You're unbelievable."

"Are you civil service, too? Or was that just a front, a smokescreen?"

"I'm civil service," Cam said wearily. "I didn't do the other as a steady diet, just took special assignments. And, yes, I want out, and they're very uptight about it. Lisa, do you realize what you've done?"

"Simply applied my gray matter to the mystery," she said, tapping her temple with a fingertip, "and computed."

"Listen to me," he said, sitting down next to her. "I was trying to protect you from all this."

"Oh, Cam," she said, sighing, "why? I'm proud of what you've done for this country, not horrified. With my overactive imagination, I didn't allow myself to start guessing as to what your secrets were, or I prob-

ably would have scared myself to death. Why didn't
you tell me?''

"You don't understand. I'm definitely quitting the
agency. In order to do that I have to be debriefed,
which means they take me in and keep me under
wraps. Because I'm involved with you, they'd pull you
in, too, but they'd figure out you didn't know anything and bring you home. As it stands now, I can't
guarantee they won't hold you as long as they do me."

"Oh, I see," she said, nodding slowly. "What about
Bret?"

"He's out of it because he already has a security
clearance from when he did those government contracts. Why do you have to be so intelligent?"

"Just lucky, I guess. How long would they hold
you, me, us?"

"I have no idea."

"But I have to finish my book. Where would they
take us?"

"I don't know."

"Would we be together?"

"I don't know."

"Some secret agent you are. You don't know anything. Can they really do this to me? I'm a law-abiding
taxpayer."

"They can do just about anything they want in the
name of national security. All I can do is explain that
you figured it out on your own and that I gave you no
details. None. I doubt they'll buy it, though. They
pride themselves on being supersneaks, and you pieced
it together as easily as a four-year-old's puzzle. You're
something."

"I guess you're not too thrilled with me at the moment," she said, frowning.

Cam pulled her into his arms, and Lisa rested her head on his shoulder.

"I'm worried about you, mad at myself, and in love with you," he said.

"That's quite a list," she said, smiling.

"Lisa, I did this the way I thought was best. I didn't want there to be secrets between us. I was so afraid you'd start lumping me into the same mold as Weber. Do you understand why I didn't tell you?"

"Yes. I could have handled it, you know, but, yes, I understand."

"Thank God for that much."

"What about your civil-service job? And Peterson Computer?"

"I haven't had time to sort even that through. I'll tackle that when this other is over with."

"But the civil-service assignments are dangerous, Cam."

"That's all on hold for now. Look, I messed it up again by pressing for action tonight. I should have been patient and waited. Then there would have been time for you to finish your book. There still might be, but I don't know. The next thing I do right, my system will probably go into shock. I can't believe how lousily I've handled all this."

"Cam, when they talk to me, what do I tell them?"

"The truth, pure and simple. Ah, Lisa, I'm so sorry I dragged you into this."

Lisa lifted her head, frowning when she saw the concern on Cam's face, the flicker of pain in his dark eyes.

"You're too hard on yourself," she said. "You said everything is going to be fine, and I believe that. I love you, Cameron Porter, my pirate. We'll get through this all right.'' Through this strange drama, yes, Lisa thought suddenly, but then what? Cam still hadn't decided on his plans for the future. He... No, they had enough to worry about at the moment.

"I think I'd better call Bret and bring him up to date," Cam said. "On second thought, I'll use the modem."

"You don't think the phone is tapped, do you?" Lisa said, her eyes widening.

"No," Cam said, chuckling. "Computer modems are just more fun to play with."

"Oh, for heaven's sake."

Cam cradled her face in his hands and smiled at her warmly.

"You are some kind of woman, Lisa Peterson," he said, his voice low. "I'm a lucky man."

And then he kissed her. Gently, sensuously, and thoroughly, he kissed her. Forgotten were the good guys, the events of the evening, and those yet to come. There was only the kiss, and Lisa responded instantly, wrapping her arms around Cam's neck. Desire swept through her, and her breasts grew taut, aching for Cam's touch. He lifted his head to gaze into her eyes.

"Hold that thought," he said, his voice gritty. "I'll be back in a flash after I fill Bret in."

"'Kay," she said, then drew a steadying breath.

Cam walked from the room, and Lisa wandered out onto the deck and sat on the chaise lounge, staring up at the star-studded sky.

Should she be frightened? she wondered. She was going to be questioned by government agents, for Pete's sake. In a smoky room with a bare light bulb? No, surely not. She'd tell the truth, the way Cam had told her to. The secrets were gone, at last. The future was still a hazy blur, but the ominous, crushing weight of Cam's secrets had been removed from their lives. First they had to face the consequences of Cam's decision to quit skulking in the shadows with the other agents, then...

"All set," Cam said, coming onto the deck. "Bret said to tell you that you did a helluva job of deduction. He also suggested that the agency could use you, but I told him what he could do with that idea."

Lisa laughed. "Well, darn," she said, "I was sitting here wondering how I'd look in a trench coat and fedora."

Cam smiled, and pulled a chair close to the lounge. He sat down, propped one ankle on the other knee, and took a deep breath.

"Salty night air," he said. "I don't think I'd ever get tired of sitting on this deck. The view, the peacefulness, it's really great."

"Yes, it is," Lisa said, "but... well, you're accustomed to moving around a great deal. Do you have a house somewhere?"

"An apartment in Washington, D.C. It's nothing fancy, because I don't stay there for any great length of time."

"I know you've had a very exciting life, Cam, but don't you ever get lonely?"

Cam laced his fingers behind his head and slouched lower in the chair, staring up at the spectacle of beauty in the sky. He didn't speak for several long minutes.

"Lonely," he repeated finally, his voice low. "I never thought about it, I guess. I was settled into a pattern of living, and just went with it. During this last civil-service assignment, which also included a detour for the agency, I found myself questioning, wondering what I was doing there. The crew got caught in a dangerous situation, and I had a helluva time getting them all out safely."

"But you did."

"Yeah. We flew back into Washington, and the families of the crew were waiting at the airport. Every one of my people had someone waiting. Everyone except me. I stood there watching them hugging one another, laughing, crying, and I had the thought that if I had been killed over there, it wouldn't have really mattered. Oh, my sisters would have been upset, but they have their own lives to lead. No, it wouldn't have mattered that much."

"Oh, Cam," Lisa said softly.

He leaned forward and rested his elbows on his knees, making a steeple of his fingers as he gazed out over the silver sands of the beach.

"You know," he went on, "I think part of my anger at that moment was a sense of futility, emptiness and, yes, loneliness. I ranted and raved about the danger my crew had been put in, and I meant it. But looking back, I realize it was more than that. I had a cold ache in my gut because I knew that if I kept on living my life as I was, there would never be anyone waiting for me when I came home. Never."

Tears misted Lisa's eyes as she looked at Cam. She wanted to tell him in a rush of words that she would always be there for him, would love him forever, that he was no longer alone. But she kept silent, watching the play of emotions crossing over his features. He was fighting a battle within himself, sorting, sifting, getting in touch with his inner self.

Lisa was hardly breathing as the silence stretched on. Cam was at a crossroads in his life, she realized, charting his future. Would it include her? Would the weight of their love tip the scale, keep him there in a world that was safe, warm, never lonely? Or would the pull of adventure and excitement be heavier, the years of that way of life count for more than their fragile new love? Was he going to leave her? He was sitting right there, next to her, but at that moment he seemed so very far away.

"I love you, Cam," Lisa whispered as she blinked away the tears.

He turned his head to look at her, and she saw the bleak strain of weariness etched on his face. He extended his hand to her palm up, and she placed hers in it, feeling the heat and strength as his fingers curled around her own. Cam got to his feet and drew her up next to him, enfolding her in his strong arms. He held her so tightly it was almost painful, but she stood quietly, feeling the tension in every inch of his body.

Time lost meaning. Then Lisa felt Cam relax as he took a deep breath that shuddered through him.

What was he thinking? Lisa wondered frantically. What road had his inner turmoil taken him down? Had he made the decision that would determine the future course of his life, of their lives? Or was he still caught in a tangled web of confusion?

"I want to make love to you, Lisa," he said, his voice hoarse. "Will you come inside with me now?"

Nothing, not one clue to what was going on in his mind. So be it. There was no choice for her but to wait. No choice, because she loved him. This wasn't a novel that she could control, whose outcome she could determine. This was real life, and it was frightening.

She might win her Cam, or she might lose him. "Make love to me, Cam," she said, her voice trembling. "Please."

Cam kissed her, a long, searing kiss, then led her inside and into the bedroom. Again and again through the hours of the night, they reached for each other. They soared to their treasured place, lingered there, then drifted back. The ember of passion was never thoroughly extinguished, and would burst into a raging flame at a touch, a kiss, a murmured endearment. When they slept, they lay close, heads resting on the same pillow as they nestled together.

Lisa woke at dawn to the sound of rain beating on the roof. A smile formed on her lips as she gazed at Cam. He was sleeping soundly, his breathing deep and even, one hand splayed over his bare chest. His thick dark hair tumbled over his tanned forehead, and his cheeks and chin showed the beginnings of a beard.

She wondered absently what he would look like with a mustache, resisted the urge to kiss his slightly parted lips, and moved carefully from his arms. As much as she would like to stay close to his warm body and replay in her mind the night's exquisite lovemaking, she had to be practical. She had a book to finish.

Lisa started the coffee maker, then showered in the hall bathroom so as not to wake Cam. A short time later she was dressed in jeans and a blue-and-white striped sweater. Because of the rain, the house felt chilly and damp, and she went so far as to put on her shoes. She settled in her chair in front of the computer with a steaming mug of coffee and activated the machine. Jasmine Peters was soon lost in a long-ago world.

* * *

Cam stirred and opened his eyes, groaning as he pulled his injured arm from beneath the pillow. He turned his head, saw the empty expanse of bed next to him, then rolled over onto his back. He heard the rain and, in the distance, the steady clicking of the computer keyboard.

As he closed his eyes again and began to doze, his foggy mind pulled him back to the hours spent making love with Lisa. Heat shot through his body, and he was suddenly wide awake. Awake and wanting Lisa.

He'd never get enough of her, he knew. What they shared as they became one was beyond description in its intensity, beauty, giving and taking. Being in love brought greater dimension and meaning to making love, greater meaning to simply being alive. He wanted to spend the rest of his life with Lisa, marry her, watch her grow big with his child. He wanted to be with her always and never again feel the cold ache of loneliness.

Peterson Computer. That was where the answer lay. Bret was offering him security and the means to create a normal existence. But could he do it? Cam asked himself. Sit behind a desk all day, confined within four walls until the clock said he could leave? And if he couldn't handle it, then what? Back to the jungles for hotshot Porter?

He couldn't ask Lisa to marry him until he was sure he could offer her the type of life she deserved, Cam decided. It just wouldn't be fair. He'd be a part-time husband at best if he stayed in his present career, and could at any given moment be a dead husband. No, he couldn't do that to her. He had to be positive, somehow, that he could make a go at it at Peterson Computer.

But first things first. Santini.

Cam swung his feet to the floor and sat on the edge of the bed. He hoped Lisa was having a productive morning on her book. He had enough guilt without messing up her writing career. Writing career. Pirates and flaky maidens. A degree from MIT, and Lisa was writing romantic drivel. What a waste of a brilliant mind. She had the ability to create computer programs that could benefit scores of people. But instead she dealt in fantasy. Who read those stories, if not people who weren't capable of dealing with reality. Why did Lisa do it? It just didn't make sense.

"Maybe Bret understands," Cam said under his breath, "but I sure don't." Lord, he mused, he could still remember his bitter disappointment when he'd realized he'd never be able to attend college. And there sat Lisa with a degree from one of the finest universities in the country, and she wasn't even using it. "Incredible," he said, shaking his head.

Cam got to his feet, stretched languidly, then headed for the shower. When he was dressed in jeans and a black V-neck sweater, he interrupted Lisa for a lengthy kiss and the announcement that he would haul her out of that room when it was time for lunch. He scooped up an armload of computer magazines, gave her another searing kiss, then strode out of the room.

"Whew!" Lisa said, checking her pulse and feeling the warm flush on her cheeks.

As Cam settled onto the sofa in the living room, he had the strange sensation that he was two separate people. A section of his being was aware that he was filled with immeasurable joy because he had found

Lisa. There was a peace within him, a warmth, a sense of being home after a long and lonely journey. He envisioned being married to Lisa, living there in that house on the silver sands. He had a hefty sum of money, as he'd never had time to spend much, and he could add on to the house, make more room for a family. Cam the husband and father. He liked the sound of that.

But another part of him was still Cam the agent, and that entity was wired, tense, watchful. He glanced often at the telephone, willing it to ring and bring the voice of Santini. He strained to hear the noise of an approaching car driving through the heavy rain. He wanted action, and he wanted it now. It was as though he were in limbo, suspended between what he had been and who he wished to be.

The rain continued to fall, and the temperature dropped even more. The beach was blanketed in a thick fog, making it impossible to see beyond the deck. They were encased in a marshmallow, Lisa declared at lunch. She'd turned on the furnace to take the chill off, laughed in delight when Cam said he could think of a better way to get warm, then returned to the computer after they'd shared a long kiss.

He wandered around the living room, stared out at the fog for some time, then settled back onto the sofa with the magazines.

The telephone remained silent, no cars approached the house, and the hours ticked by.

"Hooray!" Lisa yelled at five o'clock. Cam jerked in surprise and dropped the magazine he was reading. Lisa came into the living room, a bright smile on her face. "It's finished. Done. Kaput," she said. "They're kissing the socks off each other and declaring their undying love. The wind is up, the sails are puffed out in the breeze, and all is well.''

"Congratulations," Cam said, smiling at her. "Another happy ending?"

"Always a happy ending. Guaranteed. Tomorrow I edit and print, then off it goes to my agent." She flopped onto the couch.

"Are you too tired to start editing after dinner?"

"I prefer to do it all in one day so I have the continuity of the story. Why?"

"I'll just feel better when that book is in the mail," he said, frowning.

"One more day. That's all I need, Cam."

"Let's hope he drags his feet for one more day," he said.

Despite the inclement weather, Bret arrived after dinner, and the three spent the evening playing gin rummy. Lisa was the big winner and refused to share the chocolate chip cookies Bret swore she had won by cheating. Cam said he didn't like chocolate chip cookies anyway, then proceeded to snitch three when Lisa wasn't looking. Bret agreed to have a cup of coffee before he headed home. They moved into the living room, and Lisa sat close to Cam on the sofa. He circled her shoulders with his arm and kissed her on the temple.

"Ahh," Bret said, "ain't love somethin'? You two are enough to bring tears to my eyes."

"Oh, hush," Lisa said.

"Hey, I'm happy for you," Bret said, "I really am. I'm all for the love bug, just as long as it doesn't bite *me*. By the way, Cam, Peterson Computer got a contract today that could be right up your alley. It starts next fall."

"Oh?" Cam said.

"A big school district is hiring us to come in and set up computer labs in the high schools. We tell them what kind of equipment to buy, then our people teach the kids how to operate them, along with basic programming. It's a non-credit course, because we're not certified as teachers. That means the kids are there because they want to be, and they'll be gung ho. You could split your time between Peterson Computer and the schools and not be cooped up in an office all day."

"Interesting," Cam said, nodding.

"Think about it," Bret said. "Could be the answer to your concern about getting antsy sitting at a desk. Well, children, I know this will break your hearts, but I'm going to leave the two of you alone now and swim home. The streets are nearly full of water out there."

"I'm glad you came over, Bret," Lisa said, getting up and hugging him.

"I'll keep in close touch. Cam, do you think they'll let you call me before they whisk you out of here? I don't like the idea of you and Lisa disappearing into thin air."

"I'll press for it," Cam said, walking Bret to the door. "I imagine they'll allow it, since you have security clearance."

"When on earth are they going to make their move?" Bret asked.

"Damned if I know. I've done all I can do at this point," Cam said, shoving his hands into his pockets.

"So, what do you think?"

"Lisa needs one more day to wrap up her book. After that? I'll be ready to rattle some cages, but it's out of my hands now."

"What if you made it look like you were trying to leave town?"

"They'd just tail us. The big man is calling the shots, and all I can do is wait," Cam said, frowning deeply.

Bret shook his head. "It must be driving you nuts."

"Tell me about it. Patience is not one of my virtues."

"Porter," Bret said, laughing, "you don't have any virtues. See ya. Bye, Lisa."

"Good night, Bret," she said, then picked up the tray with the coffee cups.

Cam closed the door behind Bret, then turned. "I'll get that." He took the tray from Lisa as she passed him.

"Thanks," she said, following him into the kitchen. "Cam, what did you really think about what Bret said about the school contract?"

"It has possibilities."

"Do you think you'd enjoy working with students?"

"Yeah," he said, nodding. "Especially since they would be there by their own choosing. They'd be eager to learn."

"And it would solve your problem with sitting in one place all day," Lisa said, musing.

"Maybe."

"Darn it, Cam, can't you be more definite than that? This is important. We're talking about our . . . your future."

Cam leaned back against the counter and crossed his arms over his chest, a frown on his face. "Future?" he said. "My pie is sliced a bit thinner than that. First up is hoping for one more day of delay so you can finish your book. Then it's push comes to shove, get this whole thing over with. I'm in no position to take on decisions about my entire future.''

"I don't see why not," she said, matching his frown. "You know exactly what you intend to do about being an agent. It's over for you, finished. I see no reason why you can't look further. Wouldn't you like to have some things settled?''

"Of course I would. I'd like it all printed out on the computer with the exact days and times it's going to take place. That's one of those fantasies you're so fond of. Look, I have no intention of moving to square two until square one is old news. Why are you pushing me all of a sudden?''

"Pushing you! I happen to love you, remember? I think I have the right to know where I fit into your plans.''

"I don't have any plans past the nifty part of having you dragged in, then brought safely home. I want you back in this house where you belong. The rest of it will have to wait," he said, raking his fingers through his hair.

"So I wait, too," she said, throwing up her hands. "You may stay, you may go—who knows? I'll just sit back and be surprised.''

"I love you! Isn't that enough for now? You want everything tied up in a pretty package with a bow on top, but I can't do that right now. Would you get your head out of the clouds and face facts!''

"What is all this reference to me and fantasy, Cam? I would say I've dealt quite admirably with some very harsh facts ever since you went flying off my deck to chase your creepy friend. I also feel it is very realistic to wonder whether you're going to return to your

jungles or stay here and commit yourself to our relationship. You're allowing some men who are out there
in the shadows to control your life, and mine along
with it."

"That's how it is right now!" he roared. "Give it a
rest, will you? I've got to take this one step at a time.
That, Lisa, is my final word."

Lisa felt the tight, achy sensation in her throat that
warned her that she was about to cry. She wrapped her
hands around her elbows and stared down at the toe
of her shoe so Cam wouldn't see the tears that were
definitely on their way.

"Well, I guess that covers that," she said, her voice
not quite steady. "I'm really very tired, and I have a
tedious work day tomorrow, so I think I'll go to bed."

"Lisa, I—"

"Good night, Cam," she said, hurrying from the
room.

He swore, then turned and gripped the edge of the
sink until his knuckles were white from the pressure.
The action caused a shooting pain in his injured arm,
but he ignored it. He had hurt her again, he thought
incredulously. She'd been about to burst into tears.
Didn't she realize how concerned he was about her,
that he wouldn't rest easy until she'd been questioned, then brought safely home? How did she expect
him to think about the future before this mess with
Santini was over?

But he *had* thought about it, he realized. He'd envisioned a lifetime with Lisa, even seen her carrying
their child inside her. He'd mentally added rooms to
the house, for crying out loud. And, yes, he'd registered a surge of excitement when Bret had spoken of
the school contract. It sounded challenging, and

would give Cam some flexibility in his duties at Peterson Computer Corporation, where he had every intention of working, creating a new and rewarding career.

So why hadn't he told Lisa all those things, those plans, hopes and dreams, which included her in every aspect of his future life? It was Santini, and Cam knew it. It was a fear that somehow something would go wrong, that Santini wouldn't let him go and he'd be trapped in that other world forever. But that wasn't true. Santini had no claim on Cam's life, no power to control his soul.

How strange the human mind was, Cam pondered. He was afraid to speak aloud of the future for fear that Santini would hear and tear it from his grasp. As it was, the agency was going to touch Lisa's life, take her from her home, and that knowledge caused a twisting pain in Cam's gut. But they *would* bring Lisa home again, and Cam would be turned loose with a casual "thank you and see you around." It would be over, left in the past, and the memories of it all would dim in time.

He'd been playing mind games, Cam mused. He'd never given thought to his future before, hadn't known what to do with the heady realization that his life was his to do with as he saw fit. He'd concentrated on the here and now as he'd always done, allowing only whimsical daydreams of tomorrow.

But tomorrow was real; it wasn't fantasy. He could look further, just as Lisa had said. How he had hurt her! Cam moaned inwardly. He knew he had come across as an uncaring slob who didn't give a tinker's damn about their relationship and what they might share. She couldn't read his mind, couldn't see the pictures he'd painted there of their life together; she could only hear his words. Words that had been cold and cutting and had brought her close to tears.

"You're such a nice guy, Porter," Cam said dryly.

Cam strode from the kitchen, then slowed his step as he approached Lisa's darkened room.

He was nervous. Cute, he fumed. Big, tough street-fighter Cameron was shaking in his shoes because he had to face a hundred-pound woman. The thought of being jumped in an alley by three goons was more appealing than walking into that bedroom. Give him an opponent with a switchblade any day over Lisa Peterson with tears in her beautiful green eyes. Okay, he'd tell her that he was a louse, that he was sorry, and hope she didn't toss him out to sleep on the sofa. He could handle this.

Cam stepped into the room and moved to the edge of the bed. His eyes adjusted to the darkness and he saw Lisa huddled beneath the blankets, head on the pillow, eyes closed.

"Lisa?" he said softly.

Silence.

"Lisa, could I talk to you for a minute?"

She opened one eye and peered up at him, a frown on her face.

"Hi," he said cheerfully, then scowled in the next instant when her expression didn't change. He pulled a chair next to the bed, sat down and leaned forward, staring at that one green eye. "I...um...I'm very sorry I was so short with you, Lisa. You were right about there being no reason why I can't look further than the right now, look to the future, make plans, decisions."

The green eye blinked once, slowly. The frown remained firmly in place.

"You see," he said, wiping a line of sweat off his brow, "I'm not very good at futures, because I've never allowed myself to have one before. Before you. I love you, Lisa, and I... Well, I'm hoping you'll agree to be... That is, I'm asking you to... Would you open your other eye? You're driving me nuts!"

The other green eye popped open.

"Thank you," he said gruffly. "Where was I?"

"Loving me," Lisa said, "and babbling about something I'm supposed to do, or be, or whatever."

"Oh. Right," he said, nodding, then took a deep breath. "Lisa," he went on, his voice slightly strained, "would you do me the honor of... what I'm trying to say is—"

"Cameron!"

"Damn it," he roared, "you are going to marry me if I have to tie you up and gag you and haul you downtown to the courthouse. Understand?" Oh, now he'd *really* blown it.

A nightie-clad Lisa catapulted off the bed and landed in Cam's arms with such force that they nearly toppled over in the chair. He swung her up to sit on his lap, and she wrapped her arms around his neck.

"Does this mean you'll marry me?" he said, grinning at her.

"Do I have any choice?" she said, smiling.

"Nope."

"Oh, Cam, of course I'll marry you. I love you so much. I was miserable lying in here alone, and I shouldn't have nagged like I did, and I'm sorry."

"You didn't nag; you just pointed out a few facts. Lisa, I love you, and I'll spend the rest of my life trying to make you smile. I...you're crying? *Now* what did I do?"

"Nothing, silly man. I'm just so very happy."

"Well, don't cry about it. Tears really blow me away," he said, lowering his lips to hers.

Lisa leaned further into him, crushing her breasts against his chest as she returned his kiss eagerly, hungrily. Suddenly Cam stiffened, every muscle in his body tensing, and she looked at him questioningly.

"What's wrong?" she asked.

"Didn't you hear it?"

"Hear what?"

"Someone just knocked on the front door."

Eight

Oh, no," Lisa whispered, clutching Cam's shoulders, "it's them. Oh, Cam."

"Easy," he said, lifting her and putting her back on the bed. "You stay in here. Don't leave this room unless I come for you."

"But—"

"I love you," he said. He kissed her quickly, then left the room, pulling the door shut behind him.

Lisa scrambled off the bed and ran to the door, pressing her ear to the wood as she chewed nervously on her lower lip.

Cam was protecting her again, she thought suddenly. Thank goodness, Cam was protecting her. The last thing she wanted to do was go open the front door. He'd asked her to marry him! Everything was wonderful, fantastic, and...grim. If only it were an encyclopedia salesman pounding on their door.

Lisa cupped her hands around her ear and strained to hear through the solid door. She'd be fine, she decided, if she didn't shake all her bones loose with her trembling.

Cam opened the front door. Before him stood two men, one in his middle thirties, the other about fifty. They were dressed in dark suits, white shirts and dark ties, and their shoulders were hunched against the cold rain.

"Let us in, Porter," the older one said. "It's wet out here."

Cam raised one hand and shook his head.

"My mother always told me to never allow strangers to come in the house," Cam said. "How about a little ID, gents?"

The men produced their identification, along with stormy glares. Cam examined the cards with the careful scrutiny of one who might have difficulty reading. The younger man swore. Cam raised an eyebrow at him. Cam returned the thin black cases and stepped back.

"Well," he said, "I guess you can come in, but I won't ask you to sit down. Can't have you dripping on the furniture, you know."

"You're a pain in the butt," the younger agent said as they came into the living room.

"Me?" Cam said, covering his heart with his hand. "Why, Bob, you offend me. You don't mind if I call you Bob, do you? And you're Al?" he said, to the older man. "Bob and Al. Sounds like a singing duo."

"Put a cork in it, Porter," Al said. "You've caused enough trouble. Heads are rolling because of you."

"Do tell," Cam said dryly.

"I don't know how you managed it," Al went on, "but the man himself wants to see you and the lady. Pack some things, both of you. We're on a tight schedule."

"So is the lady," Cam said, his jaw tightening. "She needs another day to complete something imperative to her career."

"No can do," Al said. "We have our orders."

"Damn," Cam said. "Yeah, okay. I have to call her brother, though."

"Bret Peterson?" Bob said. "Go ahead, he's clear. Make the call where we can hear you, though."

"Yeah, yeah," Cam said, walking across the room. "First I want to tell Lisa what's going on."

"Hurry up," Bob said. "We're freezing in these clammy clothes."

"Most people have enough sense to stay in out of the rain," Cam shot back over his shoulder.

"I'm really beginning not to like you, Porter," Bob said.

"What a rotten shame," Cam said, reaching for the doorknob.

Lisa jumped out of the way as the door opened and Cam entered. He closed it behind him and placed his hands on her shoulders.

"I couldn't hear a thing," she said. "Was it an encyclopedia salesman?"

"Not quite," he said, smiling slightly. "Lisa, there are two agents here, and we have to go with them. Pack a few things, just jeans, sweaters, whatever. I made a pitch for an extra day for you, but it didn't wash. I'm sorry."

"I'm ahead of schedule," she said, her eyes wide. "I have some time left to get the book in. But, Cam, where are they taking us?"

"I don't know, and it wouldn't do any good to ask. Get dressed, then pack. I'm going to call Bret."

"Yes, all right."

"Damn it," he said, pulling her roughly into his arms. "You look so frightened. I wish—"

"I'm fine," she interrupted him. "Don't worry about me, Cam. I'm not going to fall apart. This will be great research if I ever decide to write a spy thriller."

"I love you," he said, then brought his mouth down hard on hers.

Lisa molded herself against him, willed herself not to cry, and answered the demands of Cam's lips and tongue. But as quickly as the kiss began, it seemed, it ended. Cam set her gently away from him, brushed his thumbs over her cheeks, then, after gazing at her for a long moment, left the room.

Lisa pressed her trembling fingers to her lips, allowed herself one deep breath, then spun around and went into the bathroom. She showered quickly, dressed in jeans and a black sweater, deciding the color was appropriate for her frame of mind, then packed a small suitcase. She had just begun packing for Cam when he reentered the room.

"I talked to Bret," he said, tossing his shaving gear into the suitcase. "You're to call him the minute you get back home."

"You don't think you and I will be returning together?"

"I hope not," he said, snapping the suitcase shut after throwing in some more clothes. "I'm counting on their realizing that you're telling the truth, you don't know any details, and they'll bring you back. Lisa, these men are government agents. They're not going to hurt you. I'm giving them a bad time simply because I'm uptight, but they're decent men doing their job. There's no reason to be frightened if we get separated, which I'm sure we will. Cooperate, tell the truth, and this will all be over very soon."

Lisa was unable to speak past the tightness in her throat, so she nodded and managed a small smile. She wanted Cam to take her in his arms once more, to allow her to feel his strength, his warmth, to hear gentle words of reassurance and love. But instead, he picked up the suitcases and gestured toward the door.

"Let's go," he said quietly.

No, let's not, Lisa thought, then opened the door.

In the living room, Cam introduced her to the two agents, both of whom, to Lisa's amazement, called her "ma'am" and politely shook her hand. Without being told, Cam placed the suitcases on the sofa and opened them. Bob went through the contents and snapped the cases shut again. Lisa gasped when Cam raised his arms over his head and submitted to a quick and expert search by Bob.

"Don't even think about it," Cam said, his voice low, as Bob looked at Lisa.

"Al?" Bob said.

"Leave her be," Al said. "Where's your weapon, Porter?"

Cam went back into the bedroom and returned with a gun, which he gave to Al. Lisa wondered if anyone would notice if she threw up. It was too much, all of it, and the sound of her racing heart echoed in her ears. When Cam handed her her coat, she stared at it as though she had no idea what to do with it.

"Everything is fine, just fine," Cam said soothingly as he poked her arms in the sleeves. "This is all routine, nothing fancy."

"Miss Peterson," Al said, smiling at her, "I apologize if we're frightening you, as that wasn't our intention. There are procedures we have to follow in circumstances like these. Cam is right; it's just routine. We're going to go for a little ride, talk to a few folks, and with any luck you'll be right back here before you know it. By the way, I'm a big fan of Jasmine Peters. I've read all your books."

"Oh, well, thank you," Lisa said, smiling. "I...I'm fine now. I'm ready to go any time you are."

Cam nodded his thanks to Al over the top of Lisa's head, then the four of them left the house. Lisa, Cam and Al climbed into the back of a van without windows in the side panels, while Bob got behind the wheel. Padded benches banked the interior walls, and Cam sat next to Lisa, taking one of her hands in his. Al sat opposite them.

"Those pirates of yours are great," Al said pleasantly as Bob drove the van away from the house. "When those storms come up on the high seas, battering the ship around, I feel as though I'm right there on deck."

"I hope you don't get seasick," Lisa said absently, glancing quickly at Cam.

He had leaned his head back and closed his eyes, giving the impression that he was totally relaxed, even slightly bored. But Lisa could feel the tension emanating from him, and she saw him straighten one finger of the fist resting on his thigh, then another finger, and a short time later, another.

Somehow, Cam was charting the course they were taking, Lisa realized with a surge of excitement. And he was doing it for her; she just knew it. He was hoping to alleviate some of her fears by being able to give her at least a rough idea of where they were. Oh, heavens, how she loved this man.

The ride continued, and so did the unobtrusive movement of Cam's fingers. When his hand was flat on his thigh, he began to fiddle with Lisa's fingers, curling one under, then another. When she left them where he placed them, he kissed her on the temple.

"Been keeping up with the baseball scores, Cam?" Al said.

Darn it, Lisa thought, Al was going to mess up Cam's calculations. Cam couldn't chat and concentrate at the same time.

"Yeah," Cam said, "I catch up when I see a newspaper. I wouldn't even guess who's going to be in the World Series. It's all up for grabs at this point. I always pick the wrong sport teams, anyway. I lost twenty bucks on the Super Bowl."

Cam curled another of Lisa's fingers under, and she shouted a silent hooray. He hadn't lost his place.

After what Lisa thought had been about an hour, the van stopped.

"I'm going to have to blindfold you," Al said. "I'm sorry, but—"

"No problem," Cam said. "Lisa, you hold on tight to me so that you don't stumble. I wouldn't want you to stumble, understand?"

"Yes, I understand," she said. She was *supposed* to stumble. She was really getting the hang of this stuff.

The rain had stopped, but the air was chilly, and heavy with moisture. Lisa clung to Cam's arm as they moved forward, their blindfolds firmly in place.

"I have my hand on Al's shoulder," Cam said. "We're doing fine."

After about fifteen steps, Lisa pretended to stumble, which she announced with a loud "Oh! I stumbled!"

Cam's arm shot out and he hauled her close to his side, bending his head and whispering in her ear.

"We're still in Malibu," he said. "Are you all right?" he asked at a normal volume. "We went in a wide circle," he whispered. "You're practically in your own back yard."

"Yes, I'm fine," Lisa said. "I wasn't sure where I was . . . going, but I feel better now. Thank you."

"Almost there," Al said. "Three porch steps ahead. They're wide, so take it slow. Easy . . . There you go. One . . . two . . . three. Ten feet to the door."

A welcome rush of warm air greeted them, then Al said they could remove their blindfolds. Lisa pulled hers away and looked up at Cam. He smiled, gave her one of his sexy winks, and Lisa's heart did a two-step.

Bob scooted around them and bounded up a winding staircase off to the right. Lisa's gaze followed him until he disappeared, then she looked over the brightly lit area. They were standing in an entryway with a crystal chandelier twinkling overhead. To the left was an enormous living room that had only one lamp burning. The furniture was covered with white drop cloths. The other doors leading off the entryway and hall were closed.

"Al," Bob said from the top of the stairs, "bring them up."

"Okay," Al said. "Miss Peterson, ladies first."

In the upstairs hallway, Bob opened a door, then stepped back.

"Miss Peterson," he said, jerking his head in the direction of the room, "in here, please."

Lisa felt Cam stiffen as he stood close to her side, and she looked up at him questioningly.

"Cam?" she said.

A muscle was jumping in his jaw, and his gaze was riveted on Bob.

"Go ahead, Lisa," Cam said, then shifted his gaze to her. "Nothing is going to happen to you. Right, Bob?"

"You have my word on that," Bob said. "Come on, Cam, quit looking at me like you're going to make mincemeat out of me. Your lady is safe here. We're not animals."

"Yeah, I know," Cam said, letting out a long breath. He brushed his lips over Lisa's. "See you soon," he said.

She managed a smile, then went into the bedroom. It was large and nicely decorated in tones of gray and rose. Settling gratefully into a chair, Lisa clasped her hands tightly in her lap, then looked up in alarm as she heard the door close. Bob smiled at her.

"Want to play cards?" he said. "Pick your game. A million dollars a point."

In spite of herself, Lisa laughed.

At the end of the hall, two men flanked a closed door, jackets unbuttoned, arms folded loosely over their broad chests.

"What do they eat?" Cam said, nodding in their direction. "Raw meat?"

Al chuckled. "Lighten up, Cam," he said, smiling. "You're so wired I can hear you crackling."

"Yeah, well," Cam said, looking back down the hall.

"Bob has her playing cards by now," Al said. "Guaranteed. Go on in. He's waiting for you."

Cam glanced again at the huge men by the door, then entered a dimly lit room that was apparently the master bedroom of the house. He closed the door, his gaze sweeping over the expanse. A man moved forward out of the shadows.

"Hello, Cam," he said.

Cam narrowed his eyes. "You're Santini," he said. "I recognize your voice, but . . ."

Santini laughed. "I'm not what you expected?" he said. "No, I suppose I'm not."

Cam frowned as he took in the man's diminutive stature, his snow-white hair, the crinkly lines of his face.

"You look like somebody's grandfather," Cam said, shaking his head.

Santini roared with laughter. "I *am* somebody's grandfather," he said. "Sit down," he said, waving Cam toward a chair. "Drink?"

"No, thanks," he said, watching Santini closely as the older man sat opposite him. "I want Lisa out of here, Santini," he said tightly.

"I'm sure you do," Santini said, looking at him steadily. "Suppose you tell me exactly what she knows. What have you told her?"

"Santini," Cam said, smiling, "that's not quite how it went. I'll fill you in completely on what Lisa Peterson told *me*."

* * *

At one o'clock the next afternoon, Lisa entered her living room and ran immediately into Bret's outstretched arms.

"I was going nuts," he said, hugging her. "I finally decided to camp out here. Are you okay?"

"Yes. No. I guess so. Oh, Bret, I didn't see Cam again after we were separated, and that was right after we got there. I won forty-two million dollars from Bob, then talked and talked with this little man named Smith, who looked like an elf, but... Smith—not Mr. Smith, just Smith—said Cam was going to relax awhile with his old friends. But they wouldn't let me see him. Smith said I'd embarrassed a lot of people because I spotted the man in the restaurant and figured out that Cam is an agent, but he said he respected my intelligence, and he also read Jasmine Peters, and... But he wouldn't let me see Cam again and... Oh, Bret," she said, and burst into tears.

"Forty-two million dollars?" Bret said.

"Bret, they've got Cam!"

"Sweetheart, they have to keep him under wraps for a bit. You know that. Let's sit down, okay?"

Lisa sank onto the sofa and brushed the tears from her cheeks.

"I'm sorry," she said. "It was just so jarring, all of it. They were very polite, treated me like a lady, but I was so frightened. I wanted to say goodbye to Cam, see him once more before I came home, but they said he was sleeping. I don't believe that. We never left Malibu, Bret. Cam was able to figure out that we were being driven in a wide circle to get to the house where we were held."

"Well, I'd guess he's not even in the city anymore," Bret said.

"Really?" she said, her eyes widening. "They've taken him someplace else?"

"I imagine they have isolated cabins or something to use to sit these situations out."

"Then all I can do is wait," Lisa said wearily. "Oh, Bret, I miss him already. He asked me to marry him, and I said yes. It's a little tough to get married when the groom's been kidnapped. I hate this, I really do. I don't even know when Cam is coming back."

"Well, maybe the days will pass quickly," Bret said. "You've got work to do and . . . you'll see, Lisa. Time will fly by."

But it didn't.

Time became an enemy Lisa had not encountered before. It mocked her with its refusal to move forward at any reasonable rate and bring Cam safely back into her embrace. Time ticked by in seconds, minutes, hours, then days. It made the nights a gloomy cave of darkness and loneliness, the days endless stretches of sunshine that refused to warm her soul.

She ached for Cam. She dreamed of Cam. She cried for Cam.

One week. Seven days.

The book was completed, and Lisa's agent called from New York after reading it, saying it was Jasmine Peters's finest novel. Lisa envisioned the pirate in the book and thought of Cam.

Lisa forced herself to stay busy. She went to the library and returned with an armload of books on the old west to begin her research for her western historical. She did a characterization chart on the tall, dark, rugged cowboy hero and thought of Cam.

Fourteen days.

Bret hovered around. He hauled Lisa out of the house for dinner, showed up unexpectedly with pizza or Chinese food, shared his chocolate chip cookies when he beat her soundly at gin rummy. Lisa's editor accepted the book for publication, and Bret took her out to celebrate.

Twenty-one days.

Lisa's research for the western was completed, the plot and characters clear in her mind. Jasmine Peters began her new book.

And Lisa Peterson ached for Cam, dreamed of Cam, and cried with loneliness for Cameron Porter.

"Day twenty-three," Lisa said at dawn one morning, staring at the calendar.

With a sigh, she carried her mug of coffee out onto the deck and curled up on the chaise lounge. The sunrise was spectacular, but she didn't care. The weather was perfect and her shorts and top were comfortable even at that early hour, but she didn't care. Jasmine had half a chapter of the new book completed, and it was excellent, but Lisa didn't care.

Lisa got to her feet and walked to the railing, propping one bare foot on the bottom rung. She gazed at the multicolored sky, the rippling water of the ocean, then the stretch of beach.

"Silver sands," she said quietly. "Oh, Cam, where are you? When are you coming home to me?"

"Lisa."

She smiled, still gazing out over the beach, savoring the memory of Cam's rich, deep voice saying her name so clearly it was as though he were there beside her.

"Lisa, I'm home."

Yes, yes, her mind whispered, those were the words she longed to hear Cam speaking. They would mean the end of the yesterdays of loneliness and the beginning of the tomorrows spent in his arms. But this was today, and she still fought her enemy, time.

"Do you still love me, Lisa? Do you still want me here?"

Lisa frowned. Why were her daydreams being so cruel? There was an edge of franticness to Cam's voice now as he asked her questions that made no sense. Wasn't she to be allowed even whimsical fantasies without pain, without tears?

The voice became a cry, a strangled moan, that sent chills sweeping through Lisa's body.

"Oh, God, Lisa. Please!"

Her head snapped around. Her eyes were riveted on the figure standing at the bottom of the stairs. She couldn't breathe as her heart pounded and a buzzing noise roared in her ears.

"Cam?" she whispered, tears suddenly blurring her vision. "Cam?" she said louder. "Cameron!" she screamed.

And then she was running.

And he was holding out his arms to her.

She flew down the stairs and flung herself at him, wrapping her arms around his neck and burying her face in his shoulder. Steel bands of corded muscle held her tightly to his hard chest, her bare toes dangling above the ground.

"Lisa, my Lisa," Cam murmured, his voice thick with emotion.

"Cam," she said, tears pouring down her cheeks. "Is it you? Is it really you?"

"Yes."

He set her gently on her feet but did not relinquish his hold on her. With trembling hands, Lisa touched his face, feeling the warmth, tracing the tanned, rugged features, inhaling the special aroma that was his alone.

"Oh, Cam, you're home," she whispered. "I love you. I missed you. You are my life."

With a shuddering moan he claimed her mouth, and a sob caught in her throat. His tongue delved deep into her mouth to meet hers, to taste, savor, rediscover. Hands roamed, touching, seeking, as Lisa and Cam pressed each other closer. Passions soared and bodies spoke their needs; her breasts heavy, aching; his manhood full, straining, heated.

Time was no longer the enemy, for time had stopped. The beach, the house, the world, the universe, all disappeared into a hazy mist.

There was only Lisa and Cam. There was only the kiss that spoke of lonely hours now forgotten. There was only want and need and desire like none before. There was only love.

Cam lifted his head, his breathing rough and labored. He gazed into Lisa's shimmering green eyes, his dark eyes unusually bright.

"I want you," he said, his voice gritty. "I want to make love to you so much. We'll talk later, I promise. But let me love you, Lisa, please."

"Yes. Oh, yes."

"Are those happy tears?"

"You know they are."

"Then I'd better get used to them, because I intend to spend the rest of my life making you happy."

"Oh, Cam, what if you're not really here? What if I'm in a daydream, a fantasy, living out a wish from my heart?"

He lifted her up into his arms. "Believe me, I'm here. And in a very few minutes, there won't be any doubt in your mind that I'm real. You heart and soul will know it and, oh, lady, I'm going to do one helluva job convincing your body. I'm home, Lisa, here, with you. And I'm never going to leave you again."

"Oh-h-h," she sobbed, fresh tears starting to fall.

"I'm not sure I can handle your being this happy," he said, taking the stairs two at a time.

Lisa laughed and nestled her face in Cam's neck as he carried her into the house and then the bedroom. He set her on her feet, then cupped her face in his hands, kissing her deeply.

He removed her top and her bra. She took off his shirt. He filled his hands with the lush fullness of her breasts. She tangled her fingers in the moist curly hair of his chest. He reached for her shorts; her hands sought the buckle on his pants. But soon they lost patience and shed their own clothing.

They tumbled onto the bed, smiling, touching, feeling, tasting. Cam drew the nipple of one of Lisa's breasts into his mouth, suckling with a rhythmic pull that matched the pulsing heat within her. He moved to the other breast with loving attention as her hands splayed over his back, relishing the bunching muscles beneath her palms.

His lips inched lower over silky skin to the flat plane of her stomach as his hand skimmed up her smooth thigh. Lips and hand met at the place of promised ecstasy, and a soft moan of pleasure whispered from Lisa's throat. Her body seemed to hum with sensuality. She was alive again, and soon she would be whole, filled, consumed by the strength and masculinity of Cam. The sensations he was creating within her were building, surging, causing her to writhe from his tantalizing touch and gasp his name.

"Cam!"

"Soon," he said, his voice harsh with passion.

Cam found her breasts again, his mouth on one, his hand on the other. She sank her fingers in his thick dark hair, urging him closer, offering more. He was strong against her, promising what she could no longer wait to receive.

"Cam, please."

He kissed her once more, a hard, searing kiss, then moved over her.

Cam was home.

He was there, and they were one, and it was ecstasy. He thrust deep within the velvety darkness that sheathed him, bade him welcome, met his driving force. Lisa lifted her hips to take all of him into her, matching his pounding rhythm. Bodies glistened, hearts thrummed, names were called aloud as the cadence increased and they went further toward the pinnacle of their climb.

"Cameron!" Lisa gasped, gripping his shoulders.

He felt her spasms and gave way to his own, shuddering with the force of his release, sighing with the depth of his pleasure as he collapsed against her.

"Lisa."

She closed her eyes as the reverently spoken sound of her name drifted over her, her arms wrapped tightly around the man she loved. Cam was home, her heart and mind echoed.

Cam pushed himself up to rest on his arms and gently kissed Lisa's closed eyes, causing her to lift her lashes and smile at him.

"Hello," she said.

"Hello," he said, chuckling.

Her glance fell on his arm, and the jagged pink scar.

"Stitches are gone," he said, seeing the question on her face. "It's fine. If I say I missed you it would be so inadequate that I don't want to use those words. I'm not sure there's any way to tell you how long these days and nights have been for me."

"An eternity," Lisa said. "Such loneliness, emptiness. I became so frightened at times, because I didn't even know where you were. I couldn't be brave for a set number of days, because I didn't know how many there'd be."

"I can't tell you where I was, but it's all over, Lisa. Finished. I'll always be sorry for what I put you through, but it's a thing of the past now. I have a message for you, by the way."

"Oh?"

"Bob says he'll pay you the forty-two million dollars he owes you at the rate of a dollar a year."

"Sounds fair. I must call Bret and tell him you're home. My poor brother has really been through it with me these past weeks. I've been a total basket case."

"Did you finish the book?"

"Yes, and the editor accepted it without requesting any changes, which is delightful. I've just started my western historical. If it hadn't been for my writing, I would have gone out of my mind."

"I guess that's what fantasy is for," he said, moving slowly off her, "to escape from reality. Come here," he said, tucking her close to his side.

"I don't escape from reality when I write. That is darn hard work, bub."

"If you say so," he said, then yawned. "Excuse me. I've been up all night."

"Really? Then you'd better sleep for a while."

"No, I want to stay awake and look at you, touch you, taste you, make love to you for hours."

"Hours? As tired as you are? Are you sure about that?"

"No," he said, laughing, "I'm not. If someone yelled 'fire' right now, I don't think I could move. I do, however, recuperate very quickly. A short nap and I'll be as good as new."

"Are you hungry?"

Cam's answer was a sexy wink, which produced a burst of laughter from Lisa. Cam's lashes drifted down onto his tanned cheeks.

"Lisa," he said, sighing deeply, "will you marry me?"

"Yes, Cameron, I will."

"That's ... good," he said, his voice trailing off. "Glad to ... hear it."

"Sleep well, my love," she whispered.

Lisa didn't move for the next half hour. She simply lay close to Cam and watched him sleep. It was a silly thing to do, she supposed, but she didn't care. She gazed at every inch of his beautifully proportioned body and allowed desire to swirl within her as she anticipated what awaited her when he awoke. She studied his face, saw the strength and authority there even in slumber. She saw the scars on his shoulder and arm and frowned, then smiled again as she realized his life of danger was behind him.

Cam was home.

"I love you," she said softly, then moved quietly off the bed.

A short time later, Lisa was showered and dressed in her shorts and top. She glanced at a clock and decided to see if Bret was still at home. It was close to the time he would be leaving for Peterson Computer, but she might catch him before he left. She turned on her computer.

ARE YOU THERE, she typed, OR OFF TO EARN YOUR KEEP?

Several minutes passed, then words began to appear on the green screen.

WAS JUST HEADING OUT THE DOOR. WHAT'S UP?

MY PIRATE IS HOME, Lisa typed, knowing there was a smile on her face.

NO JOKE? came Bret's instant reply. CAM IS BACK AMONG THE LIVING? FANTASTIC. IS THE WEDDING STILL ON?

YOU'D BETTER BELIEVE IT. BRET, THANK YOU SO MUCH FOR EVERYTHING. YOU'VE BEEN WONDERFUL.

I LOVE YOU, KID. AND I LOVE THAT UGLY LUG YOU'RE MARRYING. WE'LL GET TOGETHER WHEN YOU TWO COME UP FOR AIR. GOTTA RUN.

Lisa blew a kiss at the computer, then settled back in her chair, her mind drifting to the man asleep in her bed.

"Jasmine," she said aloud, sitting bolt upright, "get to work. Don't you realize how long that poor cowboy has been sitting on that horse? Whoever heard of a handsome hero with bow legs?"

An hour later, Lisa laughed at her own foolishness. Every ten minutes or so she'd go to her bedroom door and peek in to make sure Cam was still there. He was fast asleep, his breathing steady, one arm thrown above his head.

They'd be married as soon as possible, Lisa mused, sinking into her chair again. There was nothing standing in their way now. Or was there? There she sat assuming Cam was going to work for Peterson Computer. Had he ever really said that? No, he'd said he was ready to make decisions about their future, then the "good guys" had shown up. Oh, surely he wouldn't go back to his jungles. No, of course not. Would he? When he woke up, they'd talk about everything. In the meantime, she'd better get back to work and keep her behind glued to the chair for longer than ten minutes at a stretch.

Lisa lifted her slender fingers to the keys, then suddenly pulled her hands back to rest on her thighs, a frown on her face.

"That is darn hard work, bub," she had said to Cam in regard to her writing. What had he replied? Lisa asked herself. He had said, "If you say so," insinuating that her writing was nothing more than a convenient way to escape from reality into a fantasy land. Cam had no concept at all of how tedious, draining, challenging, her career was.

Well, no problem, Lisa decided, smiling again. The upheaval in their existence was over at last. They'd be married; they'd share all aspects of their living and loving. Everything was going to be absolutely wonderful. Cam would come to see what a writing career actually consisted of. And she already understood his world, the world of computers.

"All is well," Lisa said. "And Cam is home at last."

Nine

Cam was in the hazy twilight zone between being asleep and fully awake. Lord, he thought foggily, another evening ahead of playing cards with Bob and Al. When they finally let Cam out of that cabin, he'd never play cards again. And spaghetti. He was sick to death of spaghetti and...

"Wait a minute," he said, opening his eyes and sitting bolt upright on the bed. His gaze swept over the room, and a wide smile instantly appeared on his face. Lisa. He was home. The mess with Santini was over. The future was Lisa's and his now, and everything was going to fall into place for them like pieces of an exacting puzzle. "All *right*," he said, then bounded from the bed.

He showered, shaved, pulled on clean clothes from those he'd left behind, made a mental note to retrieve his suitcase from outside the front door, and went in search of Lisa. He found her busily working at the computer, and he greeted her by nuzzling her neck.

"Oh," Lisa gasped, jumping in her chair, "you startled me. Did you sleep well? What time is it?"

"A little after two. Had lunch?"

"No."

"We eat," he said, grabbing her hand.

"But I'm right in the middle of a sentence."

"It'll keep. Come on, fair maiden. Your pirate is hungry."

Lisa laughed and allowed Cam to pull her up into his arms. He kissed her deeply, then again, then once more. She clung to his shoulders as her knees went weak and desire licked through her with whispers of heat.

"Food," Cam said, close to her lips.

"Would you like..." Lisa started, then ran out of breath. "An omelet?" she managed to finish.

"Great."

In the kitchen, Cam made toast and coffee while Lisa folded cubes of ham into frothy eggs. Delicious aromas wafted through the air, and they hurried to sit at the table with the steaming food.

"Terrific," Cam said after the first bite of his omelet. "And it's not spaghetti. It may be years before I can face spaghetti again."

"You had a steady diet of it?" she asked, smiling at him.

"Very."

"Okay, no spaghetti for at least five years."

"Oh, Lisa, do you know how good that sounds? Speaking in terms of us being together for years, forever? Look, I'd like us to be married as quickly as possible, but I don't want to rob you of a big wedding if that's what you've always wanted."

"No, I don't like those huge productions. There's a lovely little chapel near here that would be perfect. My parents are on a world cruise and won't be back for months. They'll be a bit disappointed to have missed the ceremony, but not devastated. What about your sisters?"

"I'll just tell them after the fact. It's too much hassle for them to try to get here. They both have young children. So, we agree? We get blood tests, a license, and do it. Bret will be my best man, and you should pick someone to stand up for you."

"My friend Tracey. We went through high school together, and I've stood up for her at all three of her weddings."

"Three?"

"She has lousy taste in men. Cam, what about Peterson Computer?"

"I was going to tell you all of this the night we were so rudely interrupted by the good guys beating down the door. Yes, I'm taking the position at Peterson Computer. The school project was the clincher. It's very challenging and will give me some freedom to move around. I hope Bret didn't give away my job while I was gone."

"No, of course he didn't. He even said he hoped you were thinking it over while you were wherever you were."

"I thought about a lot of things," Cam said quietly. "My entire life, for one. And you. I nearly went crazy thinking about you."

"I know the feeling."

"Actually, Lisa," he said, smiling, "I'm marrying you for your house."

"And my silver sands," she said with a laugh. "Sure, I realize that."

"I have a stack of money in a bank in Washington just itching to be spent. I thought we might add on to this place, make it big enough for a... Well, I mean, that's providing you want to have a... We haven't discussed..."

"I love it when you're so articulate, fumble mouth," she said, shaking her head. "Are you by any chance hinting at our having a baby?"

Cam snapped his fingers. "That's what they're called. I want one who looks just like you."

"Or you. And, yes, I want to have your baby. Oh, Cam, everything is so wonderful I'm almost afraid to believe it's true."

"Believe it. Eat up, then we'll go get blood tests and rings."

"Today?"

"Absolutely. We're not wasting any more time."

"Well, I *would* like to finish the scene I'm in the middle of writing before we go."

"The pirate will be here when we get back," he said, covering her hand with his on the top of the table.

"Cowboy."

"Cowboy," he said, looking directly into her green eyes as he stroked her hand with his thumb. "Wouldn't you rather put the wheels in motion to become Mrs. Cameron Porter?"

"That sounds heavenly," she said, smiling at him warmly.

"Good. Eat your eggs, then we hit the road."

It was nearly midnight when they returned to the house. They had waited for over an hour to get their blood tests, then had shopped for rings, settling on matching bands in brushed gold. They had visited the chapel and reserved it for a simple ceremony, then met up with Bret just as he arrived at his house. He had been ecstatic about their various news flashes and had insisted they all go out to dinner to celebrate the forthcoming wedding and Cam's partnership in Peterson Computer Corporation.

The champagne flowed, and a good time was had by all. Lisa, however, had no recollection of coming home when she woke at noon the next day.

"Oh-h-h," she moaned, holding her head.

"Problem?" Cam said, all innocence as he leaned against the doorjamb.

"My head hurts. My eyes, my nose, my teeth, even my hair hurts."

Cam chuckled. "Price you pay for getting sloshed."

"I did not get sloshed. Yes, I did. Oh, well, I had fun. Didn't I?"

"You did," he said, crossing the room and sitting on the edge of the bed. "We had a lot to celebrate. And because I'm a nice guy, I'll bring you a cup of coffee and two aspirins."

"I'll be indebted to you for life."

"Would it jar your head too much if I kissed you?"

"Kiss my lips, not my head. My lips don't hurt at all."

"Got it," he said, then braced his hands on the pillow and lowered his mouth to hers.

What headache? Lisa thought dreamily.

"I missed you last night," Cam murmured, trailing a ribbon of kisses along her throat.

"I was here."

"Out cold doesn't count. Do you know what it did to my libido to take off your clothes and put that nightie on you?"

"Really? Poor man."

"Interested in taking that nightie off again?"

"Thought you'd never ask," she said, reaching for the buttons on his shirt. She'd left her cowboy with one boot halfway on his foot, she thought absently. She had to get back to work. Later.

They made sweet, slow love over and over, showered together, then ate a makeshift dinner of whatever they could find in the refrigerator and cupboards. As the sunset worked its colorful magic in the sky, they strolled hand in hand along the beach, then sat on the deck and chatted lazily about nothing of consequence. Then, in unspoken agreement, they went inside to the bed they shared to soar once more to their treasured place of ecstasy. At last they slept, sated, content, at peace.

Lisa frowned, shook her head, then pushed a key on the computer to back up the pages so she could read them once more. She'd eaten a quick breakfast with Cam, then headed for the computer room with every intention of getting the cowboy's boot on his foot and a lot more written beyond that.

Now, an hour later, she'd accomplished nothing. She'd reread the last few pages, as she usually did, to get reinvolved with her characters, but had difficulty concentrating. Cam had said he would clean the kitchen, but had done so while singing a horrendous rendition of "I've Been Working on the Railroad" at full volume. He'd then moved closer, going into the bedroom to strip the sheets from the bed and remake it with fresh ones, all done to an off-key serenade of "Home on the Range."

"A dying cow," Lisa said, gritting her teeth. "The man sounds like a dying cow."

She got to her feet and marched out of the room. Cam had his arms full of bed clothes when she entered the bedroom.

"Where the deer and the antelope play," he sang. "Where seldom is heard a—"

"I hate to be the discouraging word," Lisa said, frowning. "But could you put a cork in it, Porter?"

"What?" he said, looking up in surprise.

"I can't concentrate with that—that whatever it is you're doing."

"I'm singing."

"Don't make it your life's work, or you'll starve to death."

"Oh," he said, frowning. "That bad, huh?"

"That bad."

"Well, shucks, darlin'," he drawled, grinning at her, "that was a western ditty. Should get you in the mood to write about your cowboy. Mood music, y'all know what I mean?"

"Shh, okay?" Lisa said, raising her hands. "Just shh."

"Yes, ma'am. Whatever you say, ma'am."

"Thank you," she said, then spun on her heel and left the room, Cam's throaty chuckle floating after her.

Back in the computer room, Lisa read the pages, then began to type. The cowboy got his boot all the way on his foot.

"Lisa," Cam said from the doorway.

"Aaagh," she screamed. "I can't believe this."

"All I want to know is how much soap to put in the washing machine."

She spun around in the chair. "One of those scoops in the box. Anything else?" she said, definitely not smiling.

"Hey, what are you getting so uptight about? We agreed I wouldn't start at Peterson Computer until we'd gotten married and had a short honeymoon. You're acting as though I'm in the way, really bugging you."

"Oh, Cam," she said, sighing, "of course you're not in the way." She went to him, wrapping her arms around his waist and looking up at him. "I'm just not used to having anyone here when I'm writing, that's all."

"Then don't write until I start at Peterson Computer," he said, shrugging. "I'm sure we can find plenty of interesting things to do until then."

"Don't be silly. I have to stay on schedule or I'll never make my deadline."

"So change the deadline."

"Cam, I can't. It's written in my contract. They'd understand if I had a real emergency, but I can't ask for an extension on a whim."

"Whim? Me? Us? Spending these days together would be a whim?" he said, frowning deeply.

"Yes. No. Darn it, Cam, that's not fair. I should be working extra hours as it is because of the time I'm taking off for the honeymoon. I didn't know you'd be coming into my life when I agreed to those deadline dates."

"Well, I'm here now," he said, his voice rising, "and it sure as hell seems to me that you could pick up the phone and tell your agent, or editor, or whoever, that things have changed. Tell them you've decided to spend your time in the real world with me, instead of in fantasy land."

"What?"

"You don't need that kind of escapism anymore. I can understand why you buried yourself in that stuff after Weber pulled his scam, but that's over and done with. It's time for you to come back to where you belong."

"What are you saying?" she whispered, stepping away from him.

"We could do the school project for Peterson Computer together, don't you see? I thought about it a lot while I was gone. It would be great working as a team. Very few husbands and wives have the same careers, have the opportunity to share so much of their lives, but we do."

"No, we don't," she said, her voice shrill. "I'm a writer. I write romance novels, and I'm very good at it. I'm no longer a computer expert or an employee of Peterson Computer. You don't understand at all. You honestly think I'm playing some kind of psychological game by writing these books. You have no idea how much mental energy it takes, how much emotion, concentration."

"All of which," he said, a muscle twitching in his jaw, "should be directed toward something of value!"

The pain was so intense it was numbing. It was cold, chilling her to the bone, and Lisa wrapped her hands around her elbows in an unconscious search for warmth. She stared at Cam with wide eyes as if she were seeing a stranger, someone she didn't really know.

"Ah, Lisa," Cam said, "don't look at me like that. I'm only saying what needs to be said, and deep inside you know I'm right. Your fantasies, your pirates, saw you through a rough time, but it's over. You belong at Peterson Computer with me and Bret."

"No!" she shrieked.

"Yes, you do! We'll be together on the school project, then after we have a baby, you can work here on developing programs for—"

"There isn't going to be a baby!" Lisa yelled, her eyes brimming with tears. "Or a wedding, or a team made up of you and me for any reason."

"Lisa, stop it," Cam said, raking his hand through his hair.

"Yes, I am stopping it," she said, her voice suddenly hushed and choked with tears. "I'm stopping it before it goes any further. I won't—I can't—be part of a relationship, a marriage, where my husband doesn't respect my chosen career. I'm proud of my work, Cam, and I know what I bring to people's lives. I won't be ridiculed in my own home, made to feel guilty and worthless because of the path I've taken. Your loving me does not give you the right to stand in judgment of me and decide I'm falling short of your standards."

"All I said was—"

"I heard what you said. Every word. Go away, Cam. Go away and leave me alone."

"You don't mean that," he said, narrowing his eyes. "Once you think this through calmly, you'll realize that I'm right."

Lisa lifted her chin, ignoring the tears flowing down her cheeks. "Go...away," she said, hardly breathing.

Cam stared at her, his jaw tight, dark eyes flashing with anger. "Fine, pitch a fit. Throw a tantrum," he said. "I'll be at Bret's until you come to your senses."

As Cam slammed the front door behind him with a resounding thud, Lisa jerked as though she'd been physically struck. She reached out with a trembling hand toward her chair, willing her legs to carry her that far before she collapsed. Sinking onto the soft leather, she drew great, gulping breaths of air into her lungs as black spots danced before her eyes. Tears ran down her cheeks and slid along her throat as she stared unseeing at the glowing computer screen.

"Cam?" she whispered. It was over, shattered into a million pieces, scattered like sand when a breeze swept across the beach, the silver sands. Cam didn't know or understand her, or respect the part of her that was Jasmine Peters. She couldn't marry him, live with him, knowing how he felt about what was so important to her. They couldn't survive with his attitude standing between them. It would destroy them and all that they had together. She'd had no choice but to send him away.

And she missed him already.

And she loved him, would always love him. But she was Jasmine as well as Lisa, and he wanted only Lisa in his life. She couldn't give up her writing for Cam; to do so would be to lose a part of herself, of who she was. She had to be a complete entity before she could give and take in a loving relationship.

"Oh, Cam," she said, covering her face with her hands.

Cam ran along the beach, his pounding feet evidence of his fury. He'd driven to Bret's, found a pair of cutoffs among the clothes he'd left there, and gone out again, too wired, tense, angry, to sit still. He headed in the opposite direction from Lisa's and soon found himself skirting the occupants of a stretch of public beach.

"Hey, watch the sand, buddy," a man yelled.

"Yeah, sorry," Cam muttered, not slowing his pace. Lisa belonged at Peterson Computer, he knew she did, and so did she. She had to get out of that fantasy world of hers. Pirates, maidens, cowboys. Let the dimwits write it, and the ding-dongs read it. Lisa had more going for her than that, more to offer society, to offer him, Bret, herself.

Yeah, okay, the writing had been her salvation after what had happened with Weber, but enough was enough. Why hadn't Bret pressed her to come back to Peterson Computer? Surely he realized it was time for Lisa to give up her fantasies and return to the real world. Cam, their future, their life together, everything that mattered was in the real world. She had no reason to hide herself away anymore. He was there, he loved her, he'd protect and care for her. She would calm down, sort it through, and get her head on straight. And if he didn't stop running, his lungs were going to explode.

Cam slowed his pace, then stopped, planting his hands on his hips and staring up at the sky as he waited for his breathing to return to normal. He started walking toward Bret's. He'd had enough of thinking for now. He just hoped Lisa wasn't still crying.

"You told her what?" Bret said, his eyes wide as he began to pace back and forth across his living room. "Are you out of your ever-lovin' mind?"

"Give me a break, Bret," Cam said, none too quietly. "Surely you don't think Lisa should still be writing that garbage."

"Garbage!"

"I'm surprised you haven't pushed her yourself to come back to Peterson Computer."

"You're crazy. Do you realize that?" Bret said. "You didn't even know her then. I've seen Lisa grow, change, blossom into a beautiful, well-rounded woman, a happy woman, because of her writing. Who do you think you are? Where do you get off telling her that what she's doing isn't worthwhile?"

"She's capable of more! Yeah, okay, there's a place for everyone, but Lisa's isn't in the world of make-believe."

"I've got one question for you, hotshot," Bret said, poking Cam in the chest with his finger. "Have you read a Jasmine Peters novel?"

"Well, no, but—"

"You're incredible," Bret said, shaking his head. "You're also an idiot. Her books are in my den. I'm going out, and I won't be back tonight. Use the time wisely, old buddy. I'm not sure that you understand that your entire future is at stake here."

Cam muttered an oath as the door slammed behind Bret.

Cam went into the kitchen for a beer, decided he didn't want one, then wandered into the den to stand in front of the bookcase. With a sigh, he pulled a Jasmine Peters novel from the shelf and settled into a soft, high-backed leather chair. He frowned at the cover of the book, turned to the first page, and began to read.

Three hours later, Cam closed the book, ran his hand down his face, and drew a deep, shuddering breath. He got slowly to his feet and walked from the room.

Lisa left the deck and went back into the living room. There had been too many memories of Cam in that house, she'd decided, and she had escaped to the redwood deck. But Cam's image had followed her outside as well, bringing fresh tears to her eyes as she stared out over the empty stretch of silver sands beneath the heavenly spectacle of stars.

She had cried until she was exhausted, then flung herself across the bed to doze in a restless slumber. Dinner had been an orange and a candy bar, then the evening had stretched out into a seemingly endless series of lonely hours.

She needed Cam. She wanted him there with her, laughing, talking, singing off-key. She ached for him to hold her, kiss her, create the wondrous sensations that always swirled within her when they became one.

But she needed even more. He had to know, understand, and respect her for who she was and what she had chosen as her life's work. But he didn't. And it hurt. Oh, how it hurt.

A sudden sound brought her back from her tormented reverie.

"The modem," she said. "Bret."

She hurried into the computer room, her breath catching in her throat as she read the message on the screen.

LISA, it said, MAY I PLEASE COME AND TALK TO YOU? I'LL MEET YOU ON THE SILVER SANDS. CAM.

Oh, Cam, she thought frantically. And say what? That he was giving her an ultimatum? Her writing or him? No, oh, no.

YES, she typed with trembling fingers.

Lisa stuck her feet in her loafers and went back onto the deck, then walked slowly down the stairs and a short distance across the beach. Less than ten minutes later she heard the car approach, and stop; then the door slammed. With a racing heart she turned to watch Cam approach, the silvery luminescence of the moon and stars seeming to sweep over him like a glorious waterfall.

"Hello, Lisa," he said, halting about a foot in front of her and shoving his hands into his pockets. How he loved her.

"Hello, Cam," she said softly. Hello, my love.

"Lisa, I . . . I came here to beg your forgiveness."

"Pardon me?" she said, blinking slowly.

"It's true. I'm begging you to forgive me for being narrow-minded, for having preconceived ideas about something I knew nothing about."

"I don't understand."

"I just finished reading a Jasmine Peters novel."

"You read my . . . You did?"

"I've been such a fool," he said, staring at the sky for a moment and taking a deep breath. He looked at her again, a frown on his face. "Your writing isn't fantasy; it's life. Yeah, it's set in another era, but that doesn't change the messages I found on those pages. You spoke of true love through the good times and bad, total commitment. You spoke of the sharing, the joining of souls as well as bodies, and showed the beautiful difference between sex and making love."

"Oh, Cam," she said.

"And you told your readers not to give up, no matter what happens to them, to hang in there and fight for what they want from life. You give them hope, a chance to laugh, and the healthy release of tears. No, Lisa, not fantasy, not make-believe, but everything that is real and good and worth having. You have a gift, a rare talent, that enables you to touch people's hearts and minds."

"I—" Lisa began, then stopped as tears choked off her words.

"There's something else, too. Somewhere deep inside me, I've harbored a selfish grudge, a feeling of having been cheated because I couldn't go to college. Yet here I am with the career I'd dreamed of having. In spite of that, a part of me resented your not using your degree. Lord, I can't believe what a louse I've been."

"Cam, no, you—"

"Lisa, I'm sorry. I'm...so damn sorry," Cam said, his voice breaking. "Forgive me, please. I'm proud of you, your books, of what you give to so many. Let me back into your world. Oh, Lisa, I love you."

"Oh, Cameron," she sobbed, flinging herself against him. He held her tightly to him, burying his face in her silky curls. "Yes, I want to share it all with you, Cam. I love you so much. I thought...I was so afraid...I..."

"Say you forgive me."

"I do. Oh, Cam," she said, lifting her head to gaze up at him, "don't you see? Some people read those books and find nothing more than an adventure story about a daring pirate. But you saw it all, the underlying messages, the hopes and dreams. That means we believe in the same things, share the same values, want total commitment and love for a lifetime. Cam, thank you for being everything I knew in my heart you were. I love you, my pirate.''

''Ah, Lisa,'' he said, then brought his mouth down hard on hers.

The stars twinkled a million hellos, the waves lapped gently against the shore, and a gentle breeze drifted over the silver sands of Malibu Beach. Lisa and Cam, the maiden and the pirate, walked up the stairs and into the house, shutting the door on the world beyond the two of them.

Through the hours of the night they made love, soaring to their private place of splendor. They were one, not only of body, but of soul, of greater understanding that would sustain them through the rigors of time.

Out on the quiet ocean, shadows danced across the surface of the shimmering water, creating pictures to be reaped by those whose imaginative minds might see them.

A tall ship, sails full and billowing with gusting winds. And at the helm, standing straight and powerful, dark and strong, was the pirate, his maiden tucked safely by his side to sail the seas. Forever.

*   *   *   *   *

ATTRACTIVE, SPACE SAVING BOOK RACK

Display your most prized novels on this handsome and sturdy book rack. The hand-rubbed walnut finish will blend into your library decor with quiet elegance, providing a practical organizer for your favorite hard-or soft-covered books.

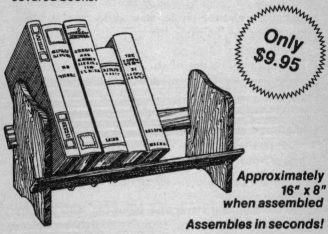

Only $9.95

Approximately 16" x 8" when assembled

Assembles in seconds!

To order, rush your name, address and zip code, along with a check or money order for $10.70* ($9.95 plus 75¢ postage and handling) payable to *Silhouette Books*.

Silhouette Books
Book Rack Offer
901 Fuhrmann Blvd.
P.O. Box 1396
Buffalo, NY 14269-1396

Offer not available in Canada.

BKR-2A

*New York and Iowa residents add appropriate sales tax.

Silhouette Desire

COMING NEXT MONTH

#367 ADAM'S STORY—Annette Broadrick
Adam St. Clair fell in love with Caitlin Moran after she saved his life.
Could he convince her that a future together was in the cards? A sequel to
Annette Broadrick's *Return to Yesterday*, #360.

#368 ANY PIRATE IN A STORM—Suzanne Carey
As the vice-president of her family corporation, Amanda Yates was fair
plunder for Royce Austin. Royce planned on a takeover, and he had more
than business on his mind!

#369 FOREVER MINE—Selwyn Marie Young
Blair Mackenzie took some time off to go camping and escape her
problems. But once she met up with mountain man Dominic Masters,
trouble was never far behind.

#370 PARTNERS FOR LIFE—Helen R. Myers
Kendall and Braden had been the best of friends and a dynamic police
team—until love got in the way. Now, no amount of danger could keep
them from dreams too long denied.

#371 JASON'S TOUCH—Sheryl Flournoy
Jason was a man of many talents, theft not the least of them, according
to Corey. But after one look at Corey, Jason was more than willing to
become a thief of hearts.

#372 ONE TOUGH HOMBRE—Joan Hohl
Though from different worlds, J.B. and Nicole were two of a kind—and it
didn't take long for them to learn that opposites attract.
This novel features characters you've met in Joan Hohl's acclaimed trilogy
for Desire.

AVAILABLE THIS MONTH:

Sarah

MAURA SEGER

Sarah wanted desperately to escape the clutches of her cruel father.
Philip needed a mother for his son, a mistress for his plantation.
It was a marriage of convenience.
Then it happened. The love they had tried to deny suddenly became a
blissful reality... only to be challenged by life's hardships and brutal
misfortunes.
